WILLIAM SHAKESPEARE

Cymbeline

EDITED BY ROBERT B. HEILMAN

PENGUIN BOOKS

BALTIMORE · MARYLAND

This edition first published 1964
Penguin Books Inc.
3300 Clipper Mill Road, Baltimore, Maryland 21211

Printed in the United States of America

CONTENTS

SHAKESPEARE AND HIS STAGE

William Shakespeare was christened in Holy Trinity Church, Stratford-on-Avon, April 26, 1564. His birth is traditionally assigned to April 23rd. He was the eldest of four boys and two girls who survived infancy in the family of John Shakespeare, glover and trader of Henley Street, and his wife Mary Arden, daughter of a small landowner of Wilmcote. In 1568 John was elected Bailiff (equivalent to Mayor) of Stratford, having already filled the minor municipal offices. The town maintained for the sons of the burgesses a free school, taught by a university graduate and offering preparation in Latin sufficient for university entrance; its early registers are lost, but there can be little doubt that Shakespeare received the formal part of his education in this school.

On November 27, 1582, a license was issued for the marriage of William Shakespeare (aged eighteen) and Ann Hathaway (aged twenty-six), and on May 26, 1583, their child Susanna was christened in Holy Trinity Church. The inference that the marriage was forced upon the youth is natural but not inevitable; betrothal was legally binding at the time, and was sometimes regarded as conferring conjugal rights. Two additional children of the marriage, the twins Hamnet and Judith, were christened on February 2, 1585. Meanwhile the prosperity of the elder Shakespeares had declined, and William was impelled to seek a career outside Stratford.

The tradition that he spent some time as a country teacher is old but unverifiable. Because of the absence of records his early twenties are called the "lost years," and only one thing about them is certain — that at least some of these years were spent in winning a place in the acting profession. He may have begun as a provincial trouper, but by 1592 he was established in London and prominent enough to be attacked. In a pamphlet of that year, *Groatsworth of Wit,* the ailing Robert Greene complained of the neglect which university writers like himself had suffered from actors, one of whom was daring to set up as a playwright:

> ... an upstart crow beautified with our feathers, that with his *Tiger's heart wrapt in a player's hide* supposes he is as well able to bombast out a blank verse as the best of you, and being an absolute Johannes-factotum, is in his own conceit the only Shake-scene in a country.

The pun on his name, and the parody of his line "O tiger's heart wrapt in a woman's hide" (*III Henry VI*), pointed clearly to Shakespeare. Some of his admirers protested, and Henry Chettle, the editor of Greene's pamphlet, saw fit to apologize:

> I am as sorry as if the original fault had been my fault, because myself have seen his demeanor no less civil than he excellent in the quality he professes. Besides divers of worship have reported his uprightness of dealing, which argues his honesty, and his facetious grace in writing that approves his art. (Prefatory epistle, *Kind Heart's Dream*)

The plague closed the London theatres for many months in 1593–94, denying the actors their livelihood. To this period belong Shakespeare's two narrative poems, *Venus and Adonis* and *Rape of Lucrece,* both dedicated to the Earl

8

of Southampton. No doubt the poet was rewarded with a gift of money as usual in such cases, but he did no further dedicating and we have no reliable information on whether Southampton, or anyone else, became his regular patron. His sonnets, first mentioned in 1598 and published without his consent in 1609, are intimate without being explicitly autobiographical. They seem to commemorate the poet's friendship with an idealized youth, rivalry with a more favored poet, and love affair with a dark mistress; and his bitterness when the mistress betrays him in conjunction with the friend; but it is difficult to decide precisely what the "story" is, impossible to decide whether it is fictional or true. The real distinction of the sonnets, at least of those not purely conventional, rests in the universality of the thoughts and moods they express, and in their poignancy and beauty.

In 1594 was formed the theatrical company known until 1603 as the Lord Chamberlain's Men, thereafter as the King's Men. Its original membership included, besides Shakespeare, the beloved clown Will Kempe and the famous actor Richard Burbage. The company acted in various London theatres and even toured the provinces, but it is chiefly associated in our minds with the Globe Theatre built on the south bank of the Thames in 1599. Shakespeare was an actor and joint owner of this company (and its Globe) through the remainder of his creative years. His plays, written at the average rate of two a year, together with Burbage's acting won it its place of leadership among the London companies.

Individual plays began to appear in print, in editions both honest and piratical, and the publishers became increasingly aware of the value of Shakespeare's name on the title pages. As early as 1598 he was hailed as the leading English dramatist in the *Palladis Tamia* of Francis Meres:

As Plautus and Seneca are accounted the best for Comedy and Tragedy among the Latins, so Shakespeare among the English is the most excellent in both kinds for the stage: for Comedy, witness his *Gentlemen of Verona,* his *Errors,* his *Love labors lost,* his *Love labors won [Taming of the Shrew?],* his *Midsummers night dream,* & his *Merchant of Venice;* for Tragedy, his *Richard the 2, Richard the 3, Henry the 4, King John, Titus Andronicus,* and his *Romeo and Juliet.*

The note is valuable, both in indicating Shakespeare's prestige and in helping us to establish a chronology. In the second half of his writing career, history plays gave place to the great tragedies; and farces and light comedies gave place to the problem plays and symbolic romances. In 1623, seven years after his death, his former fellow actors, John Hemming and Henry Condell, cooperated with a group of London printers in bringing out his plays in collected form. The volume is generally known as the First Folio.

Shakespeare had never severed his relations with Stratford. His wife and children may sometimes have shared his London lodgings, but their home was Stratford. His son Hamnet was buried there in 1596, and his daughters Susanna and Judith were married there in 1607 and 1616 respectively. (His father, for whom he had secured a coat of arms and thus the privilege of writing himself gentleman, died in 1601, his mother in 1608.) His considerable earnings in London, as actor-sharer, part owner of the Globe, and playwright, were invested chiefly in Stratford property. In 1597 he purchased for £60 New Place, one of the two most imposing residences in the town. A number of other business transactions, as well as minor episodes in his career, have left documentary records. By 1611 he was in a position to retire, and he seems gradually to have withdrawn from theatrical activity in order to live in Stratford. In March, 1616, he made a will, leaving token bequests to Burbage, Hemming, and Condell, but the bulk of his estate to his family. The most famous feature of the will, the bequest of the second-best bed to his wife, reveals nothing about Shakespeare's marriage; the quaintness of the provision seems commonplace to those familiar with ancient testaments. Shakespeare died April 23, 1616, and was buried in the Stratford church where he had been christened. Within seven years a monument was erected to his memory on the north wall of the chancel. Its portrait bust and the Droeshout engraving on the title page of the First Folio provide the only likenesses with an established claim to authenticity. The best verbal vignette was written by his rival Ben Jonson, the more impressive for being imbedded in a context mainly critical:

> ... I loved the man, and do honor his memory (on this side idolatry) as much as any. He was indeed honest, and of an open and free nature: he had an excellent fancy, brave notions, and gentle expressions. ... (*Timber or Discoveries*, c. 1623-30)

The reader of Shakespeare's plays is aided by a general knowledge of the way in which they were staged. The King's Men acquired a roofed and artificially lighted theatre only toward the close of Shakespeare's career, and then only for winter use. Nearly all his plays were designed for performance in such structures as the Globe—a three-tiered amphitheatre with a large rectangular platform extending to the center of its yard. The plays were staged by daylight, by large casts brilliantly costumed, but with only a minimum of properties, without scenery, and quite possibly without intermissions. There was a rear stage balcony for action "above," and a curtained rear recess for "discoveries" and other special effects, but by far the major portion of any play was enacted upon the projecting platform, with episode following episode in swift succession, and with shifts of time and place signaled the audience only by the momentary clearing of the stage between the episodes. Information about the identity of the characters and, when necessary, about the time and place of the action was incorporated in the dialogue. No additional indications of place have been inserted in the present editions; these are apt to obscure the original fluidity of structure, with the emphasis upon action and speech rather than scenic background. The acting, including that of the youthful apprentices to the profession who performed the parts of women, was highly skillful, with a premium placed upon grace of gesture and beauty of diction. The audiences, a cross section of the general public, commonly numbered a thousand, sometimes more than two thousand. Judged by the type of plays they applauded, these audiences were not only large but also perceptive.

THE TEXTS OF THE PLAYS

About half of Shakespeare's plays appeared in print for the first time in the folio volume of 1623. The others had been published individually, usually in quarto volumes, during his lifetime or in the six years following his death. The copy used by the printers of the quartos varied greatly in merit, sometimes representing Shakespeare's true text, sometimes only a debased version of that text. The copy used by the printers of the folio also varied in merit, but was chosen with care. Since it consisted of the best available manuscripts, or the more acceptable quartos (although frequently in editions other than the first), or of quartos corrected by reference to manuscripts, we have good or reasonably good texts of most of the thirty-seven plays.

In the present series, the plays have been newly edited from quarto or folio texts depending, when a choice offered, upon which is now regarded by bibliographical specialists as the more authoritative. The ideal has been to reproduce the chosen texts with as few alterations as possible, beyond occasional relineation, expansion of abbreviations, and modernization of punctuation and spelling. Emendation is held to a minimum, and such material as has been added, in the way of stage directions and lines supplied by an alternative text, has been enclosed in square brackets.

None of the plays printed in Shakespeare's lifetime were divided into acts and scenes, and the inference is that the author's own manuscripts were not so divided. In the folio collection, some of the plays remained undivided, some were divided into acts, and some were divided into acts and scenes. During the eighteenth century all of the plays were divided into acts and scenes, and in the Cambridge edition of the mid-nineteenth century, from which the influential Globe text derived, this division was more or less regularized and the lines were numbered. Many useful works of reference employ the act-scene-line apparatus established by the Globe text.

Since the act-scene division thus established is obviously convenient, but is of very dubious authority so far as Shakespeare's own structural principles are concerned, or the original manner of staging his plays, a problem is presented to modern editors. In the present series the act-scene division of the Globe text is retained marginally, and may be viewed as a reference aid like the line numbering. A printer's ornament marks the points of division when these points have been determined by a cleared stage indicating a shift of time and place in the action of the play, or when no harm results from the editorial assumption that there is such a shift. However, at those points where the established division is clearly misleading – that is, where continuous action has been split up into separate "scenes" – the ornament is omitted and the distortion corrected. This mechanical expedient seemed the best means of combining utility and accuracy.

The General Editor.

INTRODUCTION

In *Romeo and Juliet* (c. 1595) Romeo, believing that Juliet is dead, enters her tomb, takes poison there, and dies. Upon awaking and finding Romeo dead, Juliet stabs herself and dies. In *Antony and Cleopatra* (c. 1607) Antony, believing that Cleopatra is dead, falls on his sword and thus brings about his death. In consequence, Cleopatra resolves on death by the poisonous bite of the asp. Compare these roughly similar situations with certain events in *Cymbeline* (c. 1609–10). Imogen, recovering like Juliet from a drug which has brought about her apparent death, opens her eyes upon a corpse which she believes to be her husband's. But, though she faints, she neither takes her life nor thinks of doing so. When Posthumus receives apparent evidence of Imogen's death, he too goes on living, though he has the added burden of remorse; true, he thinks of death, but only as a natural hazard of the war that he chooses to enter.

To be sure, different lovers have different personalities. But behind the variations of personality lie literary factors that influence the strikingly different outcomes of situations up to a point strikingly alike. Different conventions are at work: in *Romeo* and *Antony*, those of tragedy; in *Cymbeline*, those of dramatic romance. As it is used here, *convention* does not mean a formula, stereotype, or constricting rule, but rather a certain point of view, a way of perceiving human behavior, of understanding it and responding to it emotionally. A convention is a bond, though a flexible one, between playwright and audience; it involves a loose, unspoken agreement about attitude and procedure; it is rooted in shared expectations, though these may be unarticulated, general rather than specific, and open to great imaginative transformation by the artist. The tragic convention interprets life as a clash between, on the one hand, transcendent principles of order and, on the other, urgencies of desire and intensities of feeling that, once they are in play, lead inevitably to destructive encounters and somber catastrophes. The convention of romance approaches life in terms of the ultimate reconcilability of desires and circumstances; though ambitions and needs may be great, they tend to fall within a realm of moral possibility; and circumstances, though they may be antagonistic for a long period, eventually yield to meritorious humanity. The tragic involvement is total, reckless, irremediable; the protagonist is wholly committed to a situation which seems to enfold all of life's possibilities. In contrast, in the convention represented in *Cymbeline* the personal impulse does not become identical with, or aspire to dominate, all of reality; beyond the individuals there is an independent life that makes legitimate claims or offers alternative possibilities. For Imogen and for Posthumus, the loved one does not become the only way, a *sine qua non;* Imogen, though grief-stricken, can cling to life, and Posthumus can fight for his country. Thus both survive for an unravelling of circumstance that offers them, in the end, satisfactions unforeseen at the moment of apparent disaster. (In the matter of circumstances romance may be contrasted with two later conventions that reacted against it: whereas romance treats circumstances as being ultimately malleable or beneficent, realism regards them as independent and subject to their own laws, and naturalism treats them as either indifferent or positively hostile to human endeavor.)

In both tragedy and romance human beings are reservoirs of strong passions. Yet romance has a greater sense of limits — of the decorum or principle or rational endowment or even pragmatic awareness that balances off the passion and holds it back from the irretrievable. Tragedy is more attuned to extremes and depths, to profound conflicts within personality (as in Macbeth, Othello, and Lear). Cymbeline, caught between the Roman Empire and British loyalty, between wife and daughter, between his dynastic plans and Imogen's emotions, is potentially a tragic figure; but Shakespeare does not portray him as destroyed by irreconcilable forces. Romance either does not see the painful inner conflict or treats it as reparable this side of catastrophe; for the clash of impulses it will most often substitute the clash of persons — sometimes simply of the good ones who come out all right in the end and the bad ones who go down. Cymbeline's Queen is all unscrupulousness; she has none of Lady Macbeth's capacity for destructive inner stresses. Cloten is self-seeking and vengeful, but as a character in romance he is not credited with the brains or drive to do permanent damage. Again, the Cymbeline-Imogen relationship has interesting resemblances to the Capulet-Juliet and the Lear-Cordelia relationships. Capulet and Cymbeline both want to impose unwelcome marriages on their daughters: in the tragedy, the father is relentless and hence contributes to the daughter's despair and to his own bitter grief; in the romance, the father is unpleasant enough, but he temporizes and hopes rather than attempts force, and hence does not push things beyond repair. In response to a daughter's independence, Cymbeline banishes a son-in-law — a sentence that need not entail disaster and that can be revoked; but Lear turns political power over to forces of unlimited ruthlessness and thus tears a whole kingdom apart.

A very clear view of the ways in which tragedy and

romance diverge is provided by the striking resemblances between *Cymbeline* and *Othello:* in each play an extremely clever man, for his own purposes, uses circumstantial evidence to persuade a husband that his new bride has been unfaithful, and the bitter and vengeful husband resolves to punish his wife by death. Though romance does not ignore evil, its vision does not include the fearful malice which, like Iago's, destroys one victim after another; instead, Iachimo's deception of Posthumus, indecent and dangerous though it is, is still a game rather than a revelation of human depravity. (Shakespeare found some aspects of the basic wager plot, a folktale that appeared in many versions, in the ninth tale of the second day in Boccaccio's *Decameron,* others in the prose tale *Frederick of Jennen,* a sixteenth-century translation of a Dutch version of a German story.) Romance may deal with a murderous impulse, but it does not give that impulse sole and final authority; whereas Othello in his mad error goes right to work and commits murder, Posthumus uses an agent who saves him from the consequences of his own fury. It may be that Posthumus is simply lucky in having to use an agent, but it is also possible to suppose that he unconsciously chooses an unreliable murderer. In either case — cooperative circumstance or secret intent — the survival of Imogen illustrates the view, almost invariable in romance, that the hate and violence of which people are capable, however great these may be, do not necessarily achieve their destructive ends.

Romance is not watered-down tragedy; it is another way of looking at conduct and experience. It is equally aware of serious dangers to life and well-being and of preventives, safety devices, the means of return from the shadows. It does not fall short of something that might be expected of it; rather it adopts a different perspective, and the better the individual romance is, the greater its ability to persuade us of the validity of its perspective. Romance can move toward theatrical (and subliterary) hackwork, or toward dramatic (and literary) excellence. Because it affirms the saving graces of life, it may either drift toward hackneyed, mechanical happy endings or struggle toward a peace and reconciliation that have been won by hard experience. (In the present example Cymbeline, Belarius, and Imogen have suffered; Posthumus has had to undergo a painful self-contemplation.) Since "entertainment" regularly plays up the comforting aspects of character and events, romance has strong affiliations with the world of entertainment: as such it can either provide standardized gratifications or require the spectator and reader to respond sharply even amid apparently familiar fare. Traditionally, romantic entertainment includes much movement and variety, distant scene and change of scene, combat, disguise, plotting, patriotic appeal. *Cymbeline* gathers all of these in a rich amalgam of many sources: Imogen's adventures in Wales may have come from an anonymous drama of the 1580's, *Sir Clyomon and Sir Clamydes;* the Belarius materials from *Rare Triumphs of Love and Fortune,* an anonymous drama acted in 1582; the political and military "history" from Holinshed's *Chronicles,* with further details from the 1578 and 1587 editions of *The Mirror for Magistrates.* Yet out of this rather astonishing medley comes not so much formula entertainment as an entertaining but not inadequate or falsifying view of reality.

After his period of great tragedies Shakespeare turned, in his latter years in the theatre, to romance: he appears to have written *Pericles, Cymbeline, The Winter's Tale,* and *The Tempest,* roughly in that order, between 1608 and 1612. Dr. Simon Forman saw a performance of *Cymbeline* at the

Globe not long before September, 1611, as we know from a description of it in his manuscript "Bocke of Plaies and Notes thereof...." The play need not have been new when he saw it, but the consensus of scholarly opinion, based upon its style and type, places the anterior limit of date in 1608–9. Certain elements in the late plays — the maturing of main characters, conversion or even rebirth, the triumph of justice in harmony with nature and divine ordinance — suggest to some readers that Shakespeare had personally come through a period of anguish into relative hopefulness and serenity. Though the interpretation is not implausible, we have no biographical evidence to substantiate it. What is established is that the romances were in tune with a theatrical fashion that grew strong from about 1608 on, representing in part the continual quest for novelty, in part a new exploitation of an older dramatic mode that had not been fully developed, and perhaps most of all a response to the more specialized taste of genteel audiences that for various reasons became influential at this time. Shakespeare was clearly writing in this new mode, but he developed the mode differently from the very popular John Fletcher and Fletcher's part-time collaborator, Francis Beaumont. Though *Cymbeline* itself and the Beaumont-Fletcher *Philaster* have resemblances that suggest influence in one direction or the other (a moot subject; the evidence is not conclusive), the Beaumont-Fletcher method is in general to decrease the seriousness of the political plot and to exploit to the utmost the private emotional life, sometimes by shocking events and strained or even morbid situations, and regularly by an intensified and prolonged presentation of feelings (pathos, shame, jealousy, humiliation, horror, and so on). In Shakespeare the situations, allowing for all the departures from every-day reality that are sanctioned by romance, are much less eccentric and much more representative, and the emotional life presented is not an end in itself, magnified for a slow savoring, but a natural unexpanded accompaniment of the action.

The customary procedures of romance, then, may lean toward either of two extremes: one, the escapist patterns and routines, where entertainment is expected to have no ties to truth; the other, a sophisticated sensationalism, where putting the audience through an emotional wringer drifts naturally toward off-center functionings of personality. Shakespeare's later romances are in a middle position: they stay away equally from the pure stereotypes that give little sense of what human character and experience are like, and from the whipping up of emotional states by strange situations and prolonged displays of exacerbated feeling.

Cymbeline has won, on the whole, less praise than *The Winter's Tale* and *The Tempest*. In *Cymbeline,* some readers believe, Shakespeare reveals a less sure control of his "later style": metrically looser lines, with extra syllables and more frequent feminine endings; a tendency toward solid blocking in dialogue, with more syntactical denseness and grammatical ambiguity; random outbreaks of somewhat mechanical riming. (There is still active dispute as to whether certain parts of the play, notably V, iv, 30–122, are authentic.) Some critics have argued that the plots are not well integrated, that Belarius is too sententious, that there are too many awkward expository soliloquies, that the characters are too neatly divided into black and white, that the gratifying conclusion lacks metaphysical support. On the other hand, few have failed to admire the characterization of Imogen and the ingenious construction of the last scene (V, v). Even allowing for the susceptibility of male critics to so charming and devoted a creature as

Imogen, whose attractions, ranging as they do from sweetness of affection to sharpness in repartee, from blind fidelity to keen insight into motives and character, from cookery to courage, make her virtually a dream girl, there is no doubt that she is one of the most substantially characterized, and hence convincing, of Shakespeare's romantic heroines. The final revelation scene, with its unbroken, energetic, unforced movement from one disclosure to another, is one of the most skillful in all drama. Unlike Fletcher, Shakespeare does not secure his effect of almost continuous surprise by playing tricks upon the spectator, keeping him artificially in the dark and then shocking him with sudden new light. The spectator, on the contrary, knows about everything that is taking place; his surprise is simply the surprise of the characters as they make major discoveries; yet he always understands the characters. His role is not that of naïve curiosity as to what is going on, or naïve wonder at novelties he has not foreseen, but adult contemplation of the diverse possibilities of human nature.

The characterization of Imogen and the management of the final scene are key elements: the merits of the play lie in characterization and craftsmanship. These reveal, as the play goes on, a view of reality that carries the romance far beyond the expectable delights of painless and thoughtless entertainment.

The play is long, and an occasional scene, such as I, iv, may be somewhat drawn out, but there is an over-all vigor of movement. Though the exposition in I, i lacks finesse, the situation is introduced, and action is started, rapidly; scenes ii and iii speedily complicate the problems to be solved. In II, iii there is a good example of a scene not only providing drama in itself but pointing ahead naturally to other action: in the midst of fighting off Cloten, Imogen misses her bracelet, so that a new problem comes into view before she is finished with the one presented by Cloten. In I, vi and II, iv, which Iachimo dominates as he first tries to "seduce" Imogen and then deceives Posthumus, excellent pace and tension are created by Iachimo in his skillful maneuvers from one strategy to another. The energetic movement is supported by variety of scene; in changing locale Shakespeare can often change mood or confront us with another point of view. From the touching scene in which Pisanio tells Imogen of Posthumus's departure (I, iii) Shakespeare makes an abrupt leap to the sophistication and skepticism at Rome (I, iv), and from that back to the heavy-handed machinations of the British Queen (I, v). The courtly polish of the scene in which Imogen, in her faithful love, resists the specious appeals of Iachimo (I, vi) is followed by the rough outdoor comedy of the loutish Cloten (II, i), and this in turn by an utterly different action in Imogen's bedroom, in which danger, evil calculation, and sexual feeling are ingeniously mixed (II, ii). From the private intrigue in Rome (II, iv, v) we are thrown back to a public scene of imperial politics at the British court (III, i), and from the royal palace to an outlaws' cave in the Welsh mountains (III, iii). From sudden battlefield reversals we shift to a supernatural vision, from divine promise to death-cell ironies, from readiness for death to a reprieve (V, iii, iv).

Nothing lags; nothing stands still; the action lines hurry on, pressed by their own inner dramatic force and intermingled so expertly that something new constantly flashes into sight to alter the perspective and undercut the obvious. This is of course good entertainment in the style of romance, but it is more than that: it is a way of countering the stereotypes into which romance may slide, of announcing the variety of possibilities in human experience, and of contemplating and accepting this variety. Though variety itself may become a cliché, variety rooted in a sense of the real alternatives in feeling and action is a denial of cliché. Even in the introductory scenes Shakespeare is not willing to let Cloten be merely the clownish butt, but instead shows him through the eyes of two commentators (I, ii; II, i), the witty observer and the straight man; aside from the drama of contrast, Cloten implicitly has enough substance to attract one follower, if only a politic one. Iachimo is the treacherous Italian dear to the Elizabethan heart, but Shakespeare modifies the conventional concept of Italian character by introducing the civil and decent Philario. The vision scene in V, iv might contain only a static, decorative theophany, but Shakespeare gives it dramatic life by having the spirits attack Jupiter almost rebelliously. Belarius and his "sons" might easily be a solid family unit playing a conventional role of rustic virtue. Belarius does voice trite sentiments about the contrast between vice at court and nobility in the mountains, but in almost their first words the young men disagree; to them their cave is a prison from the world of action and knowledge (III, iii, 27 ff.). When Guiderius kills Cloten, Belarius is less laudatory than fearful (IV, ii); when Belarius wants to play safe and wait out the war, the boys override him (IV, iv). Even the boys themselves are set partly in dramatic opposition: Guiderius, the more direct and active, criticizes Arviragus, more given to savoring words and feelings, for playing Belarius's "ingenious instrument" and for drawing out his elegy for Fidele (IV, ii).

It is in the treatment of his principal characters that Shakespeare most conspicuously avoids the expected and the obvious. As masterful wife, unscrupulous mother, and sinister stepmother, the Queen is a very old and familiar character; yet Shakespeare makes her also an authentic voice of British patriotism (III, i, v). He alters the conventional villain by giving her a generally acceptable emotion; he modifies romance by observing that malicious double-dealing at court does not bar political right feeling. Cloten is defective on nearly every count: as objectionable lover, laughable "ass," and oafish courtier of dubious principles. But he too is a patriot, even though an ungraceful one (III, i, v). He is rude and overbearing to Belarius and the King's sons, but he certainly believes that he is acting in the name of the law, and he is not a coward. His dependence on his position is ludicrous, but somehow he always needs reassurance; there is a distant touch of pathos in his incompetence and hope for security, and perhaps even in his grotesque "dreams of glory" (III, v; IV, i). He tries to think, as when he expounds the cynic's view of the gold standard in moral life (II, iii, 67 ff.), or wrestles with the paradox of love and hate (III, v, 70 ff.). In other words, Cloten is complicated enough to demand more than a stereotyped response; hence the beheading may seem excessive, unpleasantly shocking. Shakespeare wants to give the audience a quick justification for the beheading; so he has Guiderius say, "Yet I not doing this, the fool had borne / My head as I do his" (IV, ii, 116–17).

Posthumus turns out to be much more than the victim of an angry king, or than the conventional romantic hero, though he is obviously to be taken as such a hero. What interests Shakespeare more than his eligibility as a lover, or his unjust banishment, is his capacity for unheroic, indeed evil, behavior: Posthumus quickly loses faith in his wife's fidelity, and then tries to arrange her murder. Romance is made to accommodate more than a little moral reality: we see both the drive for the revenge and afterwards the bitter remorse. Imogen might be no more than faithful bride and pathetic victim, but Shakespeare gives her an intelligence, a spirit, and an imagination that make her seem to earn, rather than passively inherit, the good that comes her way. But he goes beyond even this achievement and at one point regards Imogen with amused detachment that creates the most delicately ironic scene in the play. As the convention of disguise requires, Imogen takes Cloten's body for that of Posthumus, but instead of dropping the confusion at this point, Shakespeare has her go on to identify one part of the body after another as Posthumus's. Along with all the charm of her tenderness and the pathos of her apparent bereavement, there is something exquisitely comic in the assurance of her misidentifications: no one is beyond errors that evoke smiles, Shakespeare seems to say, and this implicit view makes possible a richer humanity. The impulse to humanize by cutting back a general idealizing process appears again in the final scene when Shakespeare has Imogen coolly turn her back on Lucius ("your life . . . / Must shuffle for itself," V, v, 104–5), to whom she is indebted and who is embittered by her suddenly dropping him for her own business. Shakespeare is looking at the actual ways of human nature, not at pure stereotypes. Hence, though at the end he lets Cymbeline acquire greater wisdom and dignity, he makes the king a faulty enough human being, doting on his wife, misled, capable of folly and great harshness.

Iachimo appears first as an Italian rascal, a conventional source of agreeable shudders in Renaissance England, and then apparently undergoes a pleasing conversion from skepticism to faith in chaste love. This sounds like pure theatrical hokum, but the fact is that Iachimo is a fresh and lively character. Iago, whom Iachimo strikingly resembles, has a histrionic side which is a key to Iachimo: though Iago's main pleasure, of course, is in working out his malice, he also delights in working out the different roles that he assumes. Iachimo does not have Iago's malice, but his passion for the stage is even greater than Iago's. He loves to adopt a role and to succeed in it; he is a subtle union of actor and confidence man. Having adopted the role of disbeliever in woman's virtue, he must carry it to an extreme and conquer in it; in working on Imogen, he shifts from role to role with the agility of a born actor; in working on Posthumus, he arranges his presentation like a tight one-act play, moving from quick exposition through deepening tension to one climax and then another. Finally he chooses a very popular role, that of guilty man confessing, and here he seizes stage with an elaborate and attitudinizing self-condemnation. Even in his final five lines (V, v, 412–17) he manages to act the guilty man with a histrionic sweep, and to attract attention by praising Imogen hyperbolically.

In adopting the genre of romance, then, Shakespeare exploits all its potential variety, at one level by an always lively movement of scene and plot, and in a more fundamental way by examining characters with either an amused detachment or a fullness that stops just short of tragic complications. Though the genre commits him to solutions short of disaster, he does not impose an arbitrary happy ending. His characters are complex enough to be more than flat figures of evil that go down, and of good that triumph. The characters that survive have not been merely lucky; they have been modified, have learned somewhat better or wiser ways of confronting the unexpected. The initial mood of the play is created by a widespread impulse to act resentfully and vengefully: the Queen plots deaths, the King is quick to banish, Posthumus wants Imogen killed, and Rome must punish Britain. But the closing mood is one of forbearance and generosity. Jupiter signals the change in V, iv when, though bitterly assailed by Posthumus's family, he waives his power to act punitively and actually gives promise of relief. Cymbeline can acknowledge that his trust in the Queen "was folly in me"; Lucius can rise above the harshness of the death sentence and generously ask that Fidele be saved; Cymbeline can give up a conqueror's rights and grant this request. When Iachimo confesses, Posthumus attacks himself more sharply than he does Iachimo; by relinquishing the easier course of blame, he forestalls an outbreak of recriminatory bitterness. And if the earlier Cymbeline crops up again in the royal impulse to punish Guiderius on the spot, at least now the King can wait until he knows a little more of the truth. Belarius yields up the King's sons to their father, though he is in tears at the loss of them, and Cymbeline calls Belarius "brother." The new spirit is summed up in Posthumus, who once wanted to inflict the death sentence on his wife, but who now says to Iachimo, the cause of his mad rage, "The malice [I have] towards you [is] to forgive you." It is the key line of the latter part of the play. Moved by it, Cymbeline pardons the Roman captives and then, under the further impetus of the oracle, volunteers to pay the tribute to Rome. Since the history upon which Shakespeare drew is very shadowy, and since he follows it very loosely at best, there is no reason why he should not have chosen to finish off his romance with a patriotic note of triumph that would be sure-fire theatre. Yet he chose, not to make this easier appeal, but instead to ask the audience to respond in a more mature and less obvious way — to approve the acknowledgment of a national obligation to a foreign conqueror. Cymbeline's decision, since in effect it says, "We have all been wrong in Britain," is an act of humility. It marks the general triumph of magnanimity – the ultimate value dramatically espoused in the play.

But magnanimity is not unveiled in a last-minute surprise whose power to please depends upon our indifference to probability. It is rather an extension of a certain generousness that, though at times inactive, has been recurrently present. The court scenes with Lucius have always an air of courteous consideration that survives the political dispute ; once even the rude Cloten approaches civility (III, i, 76 ff.). Belarius, though he kidnapped the King's sons when he was unjustly banished, did not injure or kill them ; instead he brought them up in a way that could give great pleasure to the King. Belarius and Posthumus did not avenge themselves upon Cymbeline, as more persistently resentful characters might, by fighting against him in war ; instead they became the instruments of his victory. Imogen has much to forgive, but she seems not even to think of the need for forgiveness.

Shakespeare defines a world in which a certain discipline of the self – which may appear as forgiveness or forbearance under provocation, or as considerateness and graciousness even in difficult relationships – is always possible and can in the end triumph, though the impulse to inflict punishment and to achieve revenge is also strong. Civility, generosity, magnanimity – such qualities mark the improved way of life that the drama reveals. It is perhaps significant that these are the virtues esteemed in another dramatic genre that was just emerging in Jacobean England and would reach its fulness three quarters of a century later – comedy of manners. We began by discussing the relation between *Cymbeline* and tragedy (the play is entitled *The Tragedie of Cymbeline* in the folio of 1623); we end by noting its affinity to comedy. The genre to which it belongs is sometimes called tragicomedy. Whether it be called tragicomedy or romance, the important point is that, in a convention which lends itself easily to an entertaining escape from reality, Shakespeare always keeps a sure foothold in human reality; that where variety is a great theatrical value, he follows the fashion brilliantly without falling into banalities; that where abnormal tensions and sensationalism could, and often did, take over, his own portrayal of violence and strong emotion did not deflect him from representative impulses and motives; and that where the popular expectation of final relief might lead to mechanical repair of disorder and restoration of well-being, Shakespeare never entirely closes off our sense of the human capacity for ill-doing. Above all, he characteristically represents an improvement in life, not as a miraculous gift to make people easily happy, but as a possession earned by the mastery, in crises, of such virtues as forbearance and magnanimity.

University of Washington ROBERT B. HEILMAN

Note on the text: *Cymbeline* was first published in the folio of 1623. Textual scholars are divided in their opinions about the nature of the copy used by the printers, whether it was the author's draft or a scribal transcript of it, and whether this draft or transcript had or had not been used as a theatrical prompt-book. In any case, the folio text is a reasonably good one, and it has been followed closely in the present edition. The act-scene division provided marginally for reference is that of the Globe text, which departs from the division of the folio at three points indicated in the footnotes: I, i combining folio I, i and ii; II, iv and v dividing folio II, iv; and III, vi combining folio III, vi and vii. Departures from the folio text, except for relineations, normalization of speech prefixes, modernization of spelling and punctuation, and correction of obvious typographical errors, are listed below. Adopted readings are given in italics, followed by the folio (F) readings.

I, i, 4 ff. *1. Gentleman* (from here on, F assigns the speeches of the two Gentlemen simply to '1' and '2'; so also for the two Lords in I, ii, II, i, and III, iii, and for the two Captains in V, iii) 70 (F begins Scene ii here) 116 *cere* seare 143 *vile* vilde

I, iii, 9 *this* his

I, iv, 42 *offend not* offend 65 *Britain* Britanic 67 *not but* not 76 *purchase* purchases 103 *too* to 118 *thousand* thousands

I, v, 3 s.d. *Exeunt* Exit

I, vi, 28 *takes* take 98 *born* borne 104 *Fixing* Fiering 108 *by-peeping* by peeping 147 *Solicit'st* Solicites 168 *men's* men 169 *descended* defended

II, i, 11 *curtail* curtall 31 *to-night* night 58 *husband, than* Husband. Then 59 *make. The* make the 62 s.d. *Exit* Exeunt

II, ii, 49 *bare* beare

II, iii, 29 *vice* voyce 42 *solicits* solicity 137 *garment* Garments 154 *you* your

II, iv, 6 *hopes* hope 24 *mingled* wing-led 34 *through* thorough 36 *tenor* tenure 37 *Philario* Post. 47 *not* note 57 *you* yon 116 *one of* one 135 *the* her

II, v, 16 *German one* Iarmen on 27 *man may name* name

III, i, 20 *rocks* Oakes

III, ii, 67 *score* store 78 *nor* not

III, iii, 2 *Stoop* Sleepe 23 *robe* Babe 28 *know* knowes 83 *wherein they bow* whereon the Bowe

III, iv, 22 *lie* lyes 79 *afore't* a-foot 90 *make* makes 102 *eyeballs out* eyeballs

III, v, 32 *looks* looke 40 *strokes* stroke 55 s.d. *Exit* (appears after *days* in F) 138 *insultment* insulment

III, vi, 28 (F begins Scene vii here) 58 *Whither* Whether

IV, i, 13 *imperceiverant* imperseuerant

IV, ii, 49-51 *He . . . dieter* (F assigns these lines to Arviragus) 50 *sauced* sawc'st 58 *patience* patient 71 *mountaineers* Mountainers 122 *thank* thanks 154 *reck* reake 186 *ingenious* ingenuous 205 *crare* care 206 *Might* Might'st 224 *ruddock* Raddocke 290 *is* are 387 *an't* and't

IV, iii, 40 *betid* betide

IV, iv, 2 *find we* we find   17 *the* their   27 *hard* heard

V, i, 1 *wished* am wisht

V, iii, 24 *harts* hearts   42 *stooped* stopt   43 *they* the

V, iv, 18 *vile* vilde   29 S.D. *follow* followes   67 *geck* geeke   81 *look out* looke,/looke out

V, v, 64 *heard* heare   134 *On* One   198 *vilely* vildely   205 *got it* got   262 *vile* vilde   261 *from* fro   311 *on's* one's   334 *mere* neere   396 *brothers* Brother   405 *so* no   468 *this yet* yet this

Cymbeline

[Names of the Actors

Cymbeline, *King of Britain*
Cloten, *son to the Queen by a former husband*
Posthumus Leonatus, *a gentleman, husband to Imogen*
Belarius, *a banished lord, disguised under the name of Morgan*
Guiderius } *sons to Cymbeline, disguised under the names of*
Arviragus } *Polydore and Cadwal, supposed sons of Morgan*
Philario, *friend to Posthumus* }
Iachimo, *friend to Philario* } *Italians*
A French Gentleman, *friend to Philario*
Caius Lucius, *General of the Roman forces*
A Roman Captain
Two British Captains
Pisanio, *servant to Posthumus*
Cornelius, *a physician*
Two Lords *of Cymbeline's court*
Two Gentlemen *of the same*
Two Jailers
Queen, *wife to Cymbeline*
Imogen, *daughter to Cymbeline by a former queen*
Helen, *a lady attending on Imogen*
Apparitions
Lords, Ladies, Roman Senators, Tribunes, *a* Soothsayer, *a*
    Dutch Gentleman, *a* Spanish Gentleman, Musicians, Officers,
    Captains, Soldiers, Messengers, Attendants

Scene
Britain, Rome]

CYMBELINE

Enter two Gentlemen. I, i

1. *Gentleman.* You do not meet a man but frowns. Our
   bloods
  No more obey the heavens than our courtiers
  Still seem as does the King's.
2. *Gentleman.*   But what's the matter?
1. *Gentleman.* His daughter, and the heir of's kingdom,
   whom
  He purposed to his wife's sole son — a widow   5
  That late he married — hath referred herself
  Unto a poor but worthy gentleman. She's wedded,
  Her husband banished, she imprisoned. All
  Is outward sorrow, though I think the King
  Be touched at very heart.
2. *Gentleman.*   None but the King?   10
1. *Gentleman.* He that hath lost her too. So is the Queen,
  That most desired the match. But not a courtier,
  Although they wear their faces to the bent
  Of the King's looks, hath a heart that is not
  Glad at the thing they scowl at.

I, i, 1 *bloods* moods   3 *seem . . . King's* adjust their demeanor to the King's
mood or expression (cf. ll. 13–14)   5 *purposed to* intended for   6 *referred*
given   13 *bent* tendency

15 *2. Gentleman.*   And why so?
    1. Gentleman. He that hath missed the Princess is a thing
    Too bad for bad report, and he that hath her —
    I mean, that married her, alack good man,
    And therefore banished — is a creature such
20 As, to seek through the regions of the earth
    For one his like, there would be something failing
    In him that should compare. I do not think
    So fair an outward and such stuff within
    Endows a man but he.
    2. Gentleman.   You speak him far.
25 *1. Gentleman.* I do extend him, sir, within himself,
    Crush him together rather than unfold
    His measure duly.
    2. Gentleman.   What's his name and birth?
    1. Gentleman. I cannot delve him to the root. His father
    Was called Sicilius, who did join his honor
30 Against the Romans with Cassibelan,
    But had his titles by Tenantius, whom
    He served with glory and admired success,
    So gained the sur-addition Leonatus;
    And had, besides this gentleman in question,
35 Two other sons, who in the wars o' th' time
    Died with their swords in hand; for which their father,
    Then old and fond of issue, took such sorrow
    That he quit being, and his gentle lady,
    Big of this gentleman our theme, deceased

24 *speak him far* go far in praise of him   25 *extend . . . himself* expand upon his actual qualities   26–27 *Crush . . . duly* diminish his worth rather than reveal his true stature   28 *delve . . . root* dig to the root of his family tree   29–31 *Sicilius, Cassibelan, Tenantius* British rulers mentioned by Holinshed or other chroniclers   29 *did . . . honor* contributed his military fame   33 *sur-addition* added title   37 *fond of issue* loving his children   39 *Big . . . theme* pregnant with Posthumus

As he was born. The King he takes the babe   40
To his protection, calls him Posthumus Leonatus,
Breeds him and makes him of his bedchamber,
Puts to him all the learnings that his time
Could make him the receiver of, which he took
As we do air, fast as 'twas minist'red,   45
And in's spring became a harvest, lived in court —
Which rare it is to do — most praised, most loved,
A sample to the youngest, to th' more mature
A glass that feated them, and to the graver
A child that guided dotards. To his mistress,   50
For whom he now is banished — her own price
Proclaims how she esteemed him and his virtue.
By her election may be truly read
What kind of man he is.
2. *Gentleman.*   I honor him
Even out of your report. But pray you tell me,   55
Is she sole child to th' King?
1. *Gentleman.*   His only child.
He had two sons — if this be worth your hearing,
Mark it — the eldest of them at three years old,
I' th' swathing clothes the other, from their nursery
Were stol'n, and to this hour no guess in knowledge   60
Which way they went.
2. *Gentleman.*   How long is this ago?
1. *Gentleman.* Some twenty years.
2. *Gentleman.* That a king's children should be so conveyed,
So slackly guarded, and the search so slow
That could not trace them!

42 *of his bedchamber* a member of the royal retinue   43 *time* age   48 *sample* example   49 *feated* reflected flatteringly   51 *price* i.e. the price she paid   53 *election* choice   59 *swathing* swaddling   60 *guess in knowledge* conjecture leading to knowledge   63 *conveyed* taken away (i.e. stolen)

65 *1. Gentleman.*   Howsoe'er 'tis strange,
　　Or that the negligence may well be laughed at,
　　Yet is it true, sir.
　　2. Gentleman.   I do well believe you.
　　1. Gentleman. We must forbear. Here comes the gentleman,
　　The Queen, and Princess.   *Exeunt.*

　　　　Enter the Queen, Posthumus, and Imogen.

70 *Queen.* No, be assured you shall not find me, daughter,
　　After the slander of most stepmothers,
　　Evil-eyed unto you. You're my prisoner, but
　　Your jailer shall deliver you the keys
　　That lock up your restraint. For you, Posthumus,
75 So soon as I can win th' offended King,
　　I will be known your advocate. Marry, yet
　　The fire of rage is in him, and 'twere good
　　You leaned unto his sentence with what patience
　　Your wisdom may inform you.
　　Posthumus.   Please your Highness,
　　I will from hence to-day.
80 *Queen.*   You know the peril.
　　I'll fetch a turn about the garden, pitying
　　The pangs of barred affections, though the King
　　Hath charged you should not speak together.   *Exit.*
　　Imogen.   O
　　Dissembling courtesy! How fine this tyrant
85 Can tickle where she wounds! My dearest husband,
　　I something fear my father's wrath, but nothing —
　　Always reserved my holy duty — what

66 *laughed at* regarded as incredible   74 *lock ... restraint* lock up your
prison (?) lock up and restrain you (?)   78 *leaned unto* bowed to   79 *inform*
equip   81 *fetch* take   85 *tickle* (pretend to) gratify   87 *duty* i.e. as a
wife; all she fears is a divorce

His rage can do on me. You must be gone,
And I shall here abide the hourly shot
Of angry eyes, not comforted to live   90
But that there is this jewel in the world
That I may see again.
Posthumus.   My queen, my mistress.
O lady, weep no more, lest I give cause
To be suspected of more tenderness
Than doth become a man. I will remain   95
The loyal'st husband that did e'er plight troth;
My residence in Rome at one Philario's,
Who to my father was a friend, to me
Known but by letter. Thither write, my queen,
And with mine eyes I'll drink the words you send,   100
Though ink be made of gall.

Enter Queen.

Queen.   Be brief, I pray you.
If the King come, I shall incur I know not
How much of his displeasure. *[aside]* Yet I'll move him
To walk this way. I never do him wrong
But he does buy my injuries, to be friends;   105
Pays dear for my offenses.   *[Exit.]*
Posthumus.   Should we be taking leave
As long a term as yet we have to live,
The loathness to depart would grow. Adieu.
Imogen. Nay, stay a little.
Were you but riding forth to air yourself,   110
Such parting were too petty. Look here, love;
This diamond was my mother's. Take it, heart,
But keep it till you woo another wife

105 *buy* accept; reward; possibly, construe as benefits (i.e. in his eyes
she can do no wrong)

When Imogen is dead.

Posthumus.   How, how? Another?

115 You gentle gods, give me but this I have,
And cere up my embracements from a next
With bonds of death! *[Puts on the ring.]* Remain, remain
   thou here
While sense can keep it on. And, sweetest, fairest,
As I my poor self did exchange for you

120 To your so infinite loss, so in our trifles
I still win of you. For my sake wear this.
It is a manacle of love; I'll place it
Upon this fairest prisoner.   *[Puts a bracelet on her arm.]*

Imogen.   O the gods!
When shall we see again?

Enter Cymbeline and Lords.

Posthumus.   Alack, the King!

125 *Cymbeline.* Thou basest thing, avoid hence, from my sight!
If after this command thou fraught the court
With thy unworthiness, thou diest. Away!
Thou'rt poison to my blood.

Posthumus.   The gods protect you,
And bless the good remainders of the court.
I am gone.   *Exit.*

130 *Imogen.*   There cannot be a pinch in death
More sharp than this is.

Cymbeline.   O disloyal thing
That shouldst repair my youth, thou heap'st
A year's age on me.

Imogen.   I beseech you, sir,

116 *cere up* shroud (with waxed cloth; possible pun on sealing with wax)
125 *avoid* go 126 *fraught* burden 129 *remainders of* those who remain at
132 *repair* restore 133 *A year's age* (perhaps *A years' age,* i.e. an age of
years, is preferable)

Harm not yourself with your vexation.
I am senseless of your wrath; a touch more rare   135
Subdues all pangs, all fears.
Cymbeline.   Past grace? obedience?
Imogen. Past hope, and in despair; that way, past grace.
Cymbeline. That mightst have had the sole son of my queen.
Imogen. O blessed that I might not! I chose an eagle
And did avoid a puttock.   140
Cymbeline. Thou took'st a beggar, wouldst have made my
       throne
A seat for baseness.
Imogen.   No, I rather added
A luster to it.
Cymbeline.   O thou vile one!
Imogen.   Sir,
It is your fault that I have loved Posthumus.
You bred him as my playfellow, and he is   145
A man worth any woman; overbuys me
Almost the sum he pays.
Cymbeline.   What, art thou mad?
Imogen. Almost, sir. Heaven restore me! Would I were
A neatherd's daughter, and my Leonatus
Our neighbor shepherd's son.

Enter Queen.

Cymbeline.   Thou foolish thing!   150
[*To Queen*] They were again together. You have done
Not after our command. Away with her
And pen her up.

___

135 *am senseless of* do not feel *touch more rare* more painful feeling 140
puttock kite (bird of prey; a term of contempt) 146–47 *overbuys . . . pays*
what he pays (either in giving himself or in suffering punishment) almost
entirely exceeds my value 149 *neatherd* cowherd

    Queen.   Beseech your patience. Peace,
    Dear lady daughter, peace! Sweet sovereign,
155   Leave us to ourselves, and make yourself some comfort
    Out of your best advice.
    Cymbeline.   Nay, let her languish
    A drop of blood a day and, being aged,
    Die of this folly.   *Exit [with Lords].*

             Enter Pisanio.

    Queen.   Fie, you must give way.
    Here is your servant. How now, sir? What news?
    Pisanio. My lord your son drew on my master.
160   *Queen.*   Ha!
    No harm, I trust, is done?
    Pisanio.   There might have been
    But that my master rather played than fought
    And had no help of anger. They were parted
    By gentlemen at hand.
    Queen.   I am very glad on't.
165   *Imogen.* Your son's my father's friend; he takes his part
    To draw upon an exile. O brave sir!
    I would they were in Afric both together,
    Myself by with a needle that I might prick
    The goer-back. Why came you from your master?
170   *Pisanio.* On his command. He would not suffer me
    To bring him to the haven, left these notes
    Of what commands I should be subject to
    When't pleased you to employ me.
    Queen.   This hath been

---

153 *Beseech* I beg   156 *advice* (self-)admonition   *languish* pine away   158
Fie . . . way (said to Cymbeline to impress Imogen)   160 *drew on* (with his
sword)   163 *had . . . anger* was not angry enough to fight seriously   165
takes his part acts as expected   170 *suffer* permit

Your faithful servant. I dare lay mine honor
He will remain so.
Pisanio.   I humbly thank your Highness.   175
Queen. Pray walk awhile.
Imogen. About some half-hour hence pray you speak with
    me.
You shall at least go see my lord aboard.
For this time leave me.   *Exeunt.*

Enter Cloten and two Lords.   I, ii

1. Lord. Sir, I would advise you to shift a shirt; the violence
of action hath made you reek as a sacrifice. Where air
comes out, air comes in; there's none abroad so whole-
some as that you vent.

Cloten. If my shirt were bloody, then to shift it. Have I 5
hurt him?

2. Lord. [*aside*] No, faith, not so much as his patience.

1. Lord. Hurt him? His body 's a passable carcass if he be
not hurt. It is a throughfare for steel if it be not hurt.

2. Lord. [*aside*] His steel was in debt. It went o' th' backside 10
the town.

Cloten. The villain would not stand me.

2. Lord. [*aside*] No, but he fled forward still, toward your
face.

1. Lord. Stand you? You have land enough of your own, 15
but he added to your having, gave you some ground.

174 *lay* wager   I, ii, 2 *reek* give off vapors   3 *abroad* outside you
8 *passable* penetrable without damage (like a fluid; with pun on meaning
'tolerable')   9 *throughfare* thoroughfare   10 *was in debt* i.e. paid back
nothing   10–11 *went . . . town* (like a debtor taking a back road; i.e. the
rapier missed)   12 *stand* face

2. Lord. *[aside]* As many inches as you have oceans. Puppies!

Cloten. I would they had not come between us.

2. Lord. *[aside]* So would I, till you had measured how long
20   a fool you were upon the ground.

Cloten. And that she should love this fellow and refuse me!

2. Lord. *[aside]* If it be a sin to make a true election, she is
      damned.

1. Lord. Sir, as I told you always, her beauty and her brain
25   go not together. She's a good sign, but I have seen small
      reflection of her wit.

2. Lord. *[aside]* She shines not upon fools, lest the reflection
      should hurt her.

Cloten. Come, I'll to my chamber. Would there had been
30   some hurt done!

2. Lord. *[aside]* I wish not so — unless it had been the fall of
      an ass, which is no great hurt.

Cloten. You'll go with us?

1. Lord. I'll attend your lordship.

35 *Cloten.* Nay, come, let's go together.

2. Lord. Well, my lord.   *Exeunt.*

I, iii   *Enter Imogen and Pisanio.*

Imogen. I would thou grew'st unto the shores o' th' haven
      And questionedst every sail. If he should write
      And I not have it, 'twere a paper lost
      As offered mercy is. What was the last
      That he spake to thee?

17 *Puppies* vain, foolish people   22 *election* choice   25 *sign* appearance
I, iii, 2–4 *If . . . mercy is* loss of a letter would be like loss of mercy (offered
by heaven or by king)

Pisanio.   It was his queen, his queen.   5
Imogen. Then waved his handkerchief?
Pisanio.   And kissed it, madam.
Imogen. Senseless linen, happier therein than I!
    And that was all?
Pisanio.   No, madam. For so long
    As he could make me with this eye or ear
    Distinguish him from others, he did keep   10
    The deck, with glove or hat or handkerchief
    Still waving, as the fits and stirs of's mind
    Could best express how slow his soul sailed on,
    How swift his ship.
Imogen.   Thou shouldst have made him
    As little as a crow or less, ere left   15
    To after-eye him.
Pisanio.   Madam, so I did.
Imogen. I would have broke mine eyestrings, cracked them
    but
    To look upon him till the diminution
    Of space had pointed him sharp as my needle;
    Nay, followed him till he had melted from   20
    The smallness of a gnat to air, and then
    Have turned mine eye and wept. But, good Pisanio,
    When shall we hear from him?
Pisanio.   Be assured, madam,
    With his next vantage.
Imogen. I did not take my leave of him, but had   25
    Most pretty things to say. Ere I could tell him
    How I would think on him at certain hours
    Such thoughts and such; or I could make him swear
    The shes of Italy should not betray

7 *Senseless* without feeling   15–16 *ere . . . after-eye* before you stopped
gazing after   24 *next vantage* first opportunity

45

30   Mine interest and his honor; or have charged him
      At the sixth hour of morn, at noon, at midnight,
      T' encounter me with orisons, for then
      I am in heaven for him; or ere I could
      Give him that parting kiss which I had set
35   Betwixt two charming words — comes in my father,
      And like the tyrannous breathing of the north
      Shakes all our buds from growing.

Enter a Lady.

Lady.   The Queen, madam,
      Desires your Highness' company.
Imogen. Those things I bid you do, get them dispatched.
      I will attend the Queen.
40 *Pisanio.*   Madam, I shall.   *Exeunt.*

I, iv   *Enter Philario, Iachimo, a Frenchman, a Dutchman, and
        a Spaniard.*

Iachimo. Believe it, sir, I have seen him in Britain. He was
   then of a crescent note, expected to prove so worthy as
   since he hath been allowed the name of. But I could then
   have looked on him without the help of admiration,
5 though the catalogue of his endowments had been tabled
   by his side and I to peruse him by items.
Philario. You speak of him when he was less furnished than

---

32 *encounter . . . orisons* join me in prayers   35 *charming* magical, protect-
ing like a charm   36 *north* north wind   I, iv, 2 *crescent note* growing fame
4 *without . . . admiration* without feeling wonder and respect   5 *tabled* set
down in a list

now he is with that which makes him both without and
within.

Frenchman. I have seen him in France. We had very many 10
there could behold the sun with as firm eyes as he.

Iachimo. This matter of marrying his king's daughter,
wherein he must be weighed rather by her value than his
own, words him, I doubt not, a great deal from the
matter.   15

Frenchman. And then his banishment.

Iachimo. Ay, and the approbation of those that weep this
lamentable divorce under her colors are wonderfully to
extend him, be it but to fortify her judgment, which else
an easy battery might lay flat for taking a beggar without 20
less quality. But how comes it he is to sojourn with you?
How creeps acquaintance?

Philario. His father and I were soldiers together, to whom
I have been often bound for no less than my life.

Enter Posthumus.

Here comes the Briton. Let him be so entertained 25
amongst you as suits, with gentlemen of your knowing,
to a stranger of his quality. I beseech you all be better
known to this gentleman, whom I commend to you as
a noble friend of mine. How worthy he is I will leave to
appear hereafter, rather than story him in his own hearing. 30

Frenchman. Sir, we have known together in Orleans.

---

8 *makes* is the making of   11 *behold the sun* (as eagles were supposed to do;
a metaphor for distinction; cf. I, i, 139–40)   14–15 *words … matter* gives
an account of him that goes beyond the facts   18 *under her colors* as supporters of Imogen   18–19 *are … him* have the effect of greatly enlarging
his reputation   19 *fortify* justify   20 *without* i.e. with (in effect, a double
negative, found more than once in Shakespeare)   21 *quality* rank
22 *creeps* (suggests 'worming his way in')   30 *story* tell about   31 *known*
together been acquainted

Posthumus. Since when I have been debtor to you for cour-
tesies which I will be ever to pay and yet pay still.

Frenchman. Sir, you o'errate my poor kindness. I was glad
35   I did atone my countryman and you. It had been pity
you should have been put together with so mortal a purpose as then each bore, upon importance of so slight and
trivial a nature.

Posthumus. By your pardon, sir, I was then a young trav-
40   eller; rather shunned to go even with what I heard than
in my every action to be guided by others' experiences.
But upon my mended judgment, if I offend not to say it
is mended, my quarrel was not altogether slight.

Frenchman. Faith, yes, to be put to the arbitrement of
45   swords, and by such two that would by all likelihood
have confounded one the other or have fall'n both.

Iachimo. Can we with manners ask what was the difference?

Frenchman. Safely, I think. 'Twas a contention in public,
which may without contradiction suffer the report. It
50   was much like an argument that fell out last night, where
each of us fell in praise of our country mistresses; this
gentleman at that time vouching — and upon warrant of
bloody affirmation — his to be more fair, virtuous, wise,
chaste, constant, qualified, and less attemptable than any
55   the rarest of our ladies in France.

Iachimo. That lady is not now living, or this gentleman's
opinion, by this, worn out.

---

35 *atone* reconcile   36 *put together* i.e. in a duel   37 *importance* a matter
40 *shunned . . . even* declined to agree (cf. 'go along with')   42 *mended*
improved   44 *arbitrement* settlement   46 *confounded* destroyed   49 *without . . . report* without objection be reported   51 *our country mistresses* loved
women of our countries (cf. Partridge, *Shakespeare's Bawdy*, p. 95)
52–53 *warrant . . . affirmation* pledge to support by shedding blood   54 *qualified* having good qualities   *attemptable* vulnerable to seduction   57 *by . . .
out* by now not sound

Posthumus. She holds her virtue still, and I my mind.

Iachimo. You must not so far prefer her 'fore ours of Italy.

Posthumus. Being so far provoked as I was in France, I 60
would abate her nothing, though I profess myself her
adorer, not her friend.

Iachimo. As fair and as good — a kind of hand-in-hand
comparison — had been something too fair and too good
for any lady in Britain. If she went before others I have 65
seen as that diamond of yours outlusters many I have
beheld, I could not but believe she excelled many; but
I have not seen the most precious diamond that is, nor
you the lady.

Posthumus. I praised her as I rated her. So do I my stone. 70

Iachimo. What do you esteem it at?

Posthumus. More than the world enjoys.

Iachimo. Either your unparagoned mistress is dead, or she's
outprized by a trifle.

Posthumus. You are mistaken. The one may be sold or 75
given, or if there were wealth enough for the purchase
or merit for the gift. The other is not a thing for sale,
and only the gift of the gods.

Iachimo. Which the gods have given you?

Posthumus. Which by their graces I will keep. 80

Iachimo. You may wear her in title yours, but you know
strange fowl light upon neighboring ponds. Your ring
may be stol'n too. So your brace of unprizable estimations, the one is but frail and the other casual. A cunning

58 *mind* opinion   61 *abate her* lower her value (cf. 'downgrade')   62 *friend*
lover, i.e. paramour   63 *hand-in-hand* claiming equality   65 *went before*
were superior to   70 *rated* estimated   72 *enjoys* possesses   74 *outprized* sur-
passed in value   76 *or if* either if   81 *wear . . . title* have title to her, possess
her in name   82 *ponds, ring* (see Partridge, *op. cit.*, pp. 169, 179)   83–84 *unprizable estimations* inestimable values (cf. 'prize possessions')   84 *casual*
open to accident (cf. 'casualty')

85   thief, or a that-way-accomplished courtier, would hazard
the winning both of first and last.

Posthumus. Your Italy contains none so accomplished a
courtier to convince the honor of my mistress, if, in the
holding or loss of that, you term her frail. I do nothing
90   doubt you have store of thieves; notwithstanding, I fear
not my ring.

Philario. Let us leave here, gentlemen.

Posthumus. Sir, with all my heart. This worthy signior, I
thank him, makes no stranger of me; we are familiar at
95   first.

Iachimo. With five times so much conversation I should get
ground of your fair mistress, make her go back even to
the yielding, had I admittance, and opportunity to friend.

Posthumus. No, no.

100 *Iachimo.* I dare thereupon pawn the moiety of my estate to
your ring, which in my opinion o'ervalues it something.
But I make my wager rather against your confidence
than her reputation; and, to bar your offense herein too,
I durst attempt it against any lady in the world.

105 *Posthumus.* You are a great deal abused in too bold a persuasion, and I doubt not you sustain what y'are worthy
of by your attempt.

Iachimo. What's that?

Posthumus. A repulse—though your attempt, as you call it,
110   deserve more: a punishment too.

Philario. Gentlemen, enough of this. It came in too suddenly; let it die as it was born, and I pray you be better
acquainted.

88 *to convince* as to overcome (perhaps 'convict') *honor* chastity 92 *leave*
leave off (drop the subject) 94–95 *familiar at first* on easy terms from the
first 96–98 *get ground, go back, yielding* (military and duelling terms as
metaphors for sex) 98 *to* as a 100 *moiety* half 105 *abused* deceived
105–6 *persuasion* opinion 106 *sustain* will receive

Iachimo. Would I had put my estate and my neighbor's on
th' approbation of what I have spoke!   115

Posthumus. What lady would you choose to assail?

Iachimo. Yours, whom in constancy you think stands so
safe. I will lay you ten thousand ducats to your ring that,
commend me to the court where your lady is, with no
more advantage than the opportunity of a second confer-   120
ence, and I will bring from thence that honor of hers
which you imagine so reserved.

Posthumus. I will wage against your gold, gold to it. My
ring I hold dear as my finger; 'tis part of it.

Iachimo. You are a friend, and therein the wiser. If you buy 125
ladies' flesh at a million a dram, you cannot preserve it
from tainting. But I see you have some religion in you,
that you fear.

Posthumus. This is but a custom in your tongue. You bear
a graver purpose, I hope.   130

Iachimo. I am the master of my speeches, and would undergo what's spoken, I swear.

Posthumus. Will you? I shall but lend my diamond till your
return. Let there be covenants drawn between's. My
mistress exceeds in goodness the hugeness of your un- 135
worthy thinking. I dare you to this match: here's my
ring.

Philario. I will have it no lay.

Iachimo. By the gods, it is one. If I bring you no sufficient
testimony that I have enjoyed the dearest bodily part of 140

114 *put* bet 114–15 *on th' approbation of* that I can prove 119 *commend me*
recommend me, give me an introduction 120–21 *conference* meeting 122
reserved secure 123 *wage* wager *gold to it* gold in equal amount (?) 125
You . . . wiser i.e. you know her well enough to know the danger of such a
bet 127 *religion* (Iachimo sneers) 128 *that* since 129 *This* the bet, the
point of view 131–32 *undergo* undertake 134 *covenants* terms of agreement 138 *lay* wager

your mistress, my ten thousand ducats are yours; so is
your diamond too. If I come off and leave her in such
honor as you have trust in, she your jewel, this your
jewel, and my gold are yours — provided I have your
145   commendation for my more free entertainment.

Posthumus. I embrace these conditions. Let us have articles
betwixt us. Only, thus far you shall answer: if you make
your voyage upon her and give me directly to understand you have prevailed, I am no further your enemy;
150   she is not worth our debate. If she remain unseduced,
you not making it appear otherwise, for your ill opinion
and the assault you have made to her chastity you shall
answer me with your sword.

Iachimo. Your hand; a covenant. We will have these things
155   set down by lawful counsel, and straight away for Britain,
lest the bargain should catch cold and starve. I will fetch
my gold and have our two wagers recorded.

Posthumus. Agreed.   *[Exeunt Posthumus and Iachimo.]*

Frenchman. Will this hold, think you?

160 *Philario.* Signior Iachimo will not from it. Pray let us
follow 'em.   *Exeunt.*

I, v   *Enter Queen, Ladies, and Cornelius.*

Queen. Whiles yet the dew 's on ground, gather those
flowers.
Make haste. Who has the note of them?

Lady.   I, madam.

---

145 *commendation* recommendation, introduction *free entertainment* easy
reception 146 *embrace* accept *articles* terms (of the bet) 148 *voyage*
predatory expedition (with sexual innuendo) *directly* straightforwardly,
convincingly 156 *starve* die 160 *from it* give it up I, v, 2 *note* list

Queen. Dispatch.   *Exeunt Ladies.*
    Now, Master Doctor, have you brought those drugs?
Cornelius. Pleaseth your Highness, ay. Here they are,
    madam.   *[Presents a box.]* 5
    But I beseech your Grace, without offense —
    My conscience bids me ask — wherefore you have
    Commanded of me these most poisonous compounds,
    Which are the movers of a languishing death,
    But though slow, deadly.
Queen.   I wonder, Doctor,   10
    Thou ask'st me such a question. Have I not been
    Thy pupil long? Hast thou not learned me how
    To make perfumes? distil? preserve? yea, so
    That our great king himself doth woo me oft
    For my confections? Having thus far proceeded —   15
    Unless thou think'st me devilish — is't not meet
    That I did amplify my judgment in
    Other conclusions? I will try the forces
    Of these thy compounds on such creatures as
    We count not worth the hanging — but none human —   20
    To try the vigor of them and apply
    Allayments to their act, and by them gather
    Their several virtues and effects.
Cornelius.   Your Highness
    Shall from this practice but make hard your heart.
    Besides, the seeing these effects will be   25
    But noisome and infectious.
Queen.   O, content thee.

---

3 *Dispatch* do it quickly 9 *are ... of* cause 12 *learned* taught 15 *confections* compounds (drugs) 16 *meet* fitting 17 *amplify my judgment* increase my knowledge 18 *conclusions* experiments 22 *Allayments* antidotes *act* action *gather* put together (a record of) 26 *content thee* don't worry

Enter Pisanio.

[*Aside*] Here comes a flattering rascal. Upon him
Will I first work. He's for his master,
And enemy to my son. — How now, Pisanio?
30   Doctor, your service for this time is ended;
Take your own way.
Cornelius.   [*aside*] I do suspect you, madam,
But you shall do no harm.
Queen.   [*to Pisanio*] Hark thee, a word.
Cornelius. [*aside*] I do not like her. She doth think she has
Strange ling'ring poisons. I do know her spirit
35   And will not trust one of her malice with
A drug of such damned nature. Those she has
Will stupefy and dull the sense awhile,
Which first perchance she'll prove on cats and dogs,
Then afterward up higher; but there is
40   No danger in what show of death it makes,
More than the locking up the spirits a time,
To be more fresh, reviving. She is fooled
With a most false effect, and I the truer
So to be false with her.
Queen.   No further service, Doctor,
Until I send for thee.
45 *Cornelius.*   I humbly take my leave.   *Exit.*
Queen. Weeps she still, say'st thou? Dost thou think in time
She will not quench and let instructions enter
Where folly now possesses? Do thou work.
When thou shalt bring me word she loves my son,
50   I'll tell thee on the instant thou art then
As great as is thy master; greater, for
His fortunes all lie speechless and his name

47 *quench* cool down   *instructions* admonitions

Is at last gasp. Return he cannot nor
Continue where he is. To shift his being
Is to exchange one misery with another,   55
And every day that comes comes to decay
A day's work in him. What shalt thou expect
To be depender on a thing that leans,
Who cannot be new built, nor has no friends
So much as but to prop him?

                    [Drops the box. Pisanio picks it up.]
                              Thou tak'st up   60
Thou know'st not what, but take it for thy labor.
It is a thing I made which hath the King
Five times redeemed from death. I do not know
What is more cordial. Nay, I prithee take it.
It is an earnest of a farther good   65
That I mean to thee. Tell thy mistress how
The case stands with her; do't as from thyself.
Think what a chance thou changest on, but think
Thou hast thy mistress still — to boot, my son,
Who shall take notice of thee. I'll move the King   70
To any shape of thy preferment such
As thou'lt desire; and then myself, I chiefly,
That set thee on to this desert, am bound
To load thy merit richly. Call my women.
Think on my words.   *Exit Pisanio.*
                    A sly and constant knave,   75
Not to be shaked; the agent for his master,
And the remembrancer of her to hold

54 *being* abode   56–57 *comes to . . . him* brings a day to nought for him
58 *leans* begins to fall   64 *cordial* restorative   65 *earnest* sample; token payment   66 *mean to* intend for   68 *chance . . . on* good chance (this is) to
change (service)   71 *shape . . . preferment* kind of advancement   73 *desert*
meritorious action   74 *load* reward   76 *shaked* shaken (in his devotion to
Posthumus)   77 *remembrancer* agent whose duty is to remind (legal term)

The handfast to her lord. I have given him that
Which, if he take, shall quite unpeople her
80   Of liegers for her sweet, and which she after,
Except she bend her humor, shall be assured
To taste of too.

Enter Pisanio and Ladies.

              So, so. Well done, well done.
The violets, cowslips, and the primroses
Bear to my closet. Fare thee well, Pisanio.
Think on my words.   *Exit Queen, and Ladies.*
85 *Pisanio.*   And shall do.
But when to my good lord I prove untrue,
I'll choke myself. There's all I'll do for you.   *Exit.*

I, vi   *Enter Imogen alone.*

Imogen. A father cruel and a stepdame false,
A foolish suitor to a wedded lady
That hath her husband banished. O, that husband,
My supreme crown of grief, and those repeated
5   Vexations of it! Had I been thief-stol'n,
As my two brothers, happy; but most miserable
Is the desire that's glorious. Blessed be those,
How mean soe'er, that have their honest wills,
Which seasons comfort. Who may this be? Fie!

78 *handfast* marriage contract   80 *liegers . . . sweet* her husband's ambassadors   81 *bend her humor* change her mind   82 *So, so* good   84 *closet* room
I, vi, 4 *repeated* which I have recounted (in ll. 1–3)   7 *glorious* for a noble
thing (?) held by a person in high position (?)   8 *honest wills* plain desires
9 *seasons* adds relish to

Enter Pisanio and Iachimo.

Pisanio. Madam, a noble gentleman of Rome   10
  Comes from my lord with letters.
Iachimo.   Change you, madam:
  The worthy Leonatus is in safety
  And greets your Highness dearly.   *[Presents a letter.]*
Imogen.   Thanks, good sir.
  You're kindly welcome.
Iachimo. [aside] All of her that is out of door most rich!   15
  If she be furnished with a mind so rare,
  She is alone th' Arabian bird, and I
  Have lost the wager. Boldness be my friend!
  Arm me, audacity, from head to foot,
  Or like the Parthian I shall flying fight –   20
  Rather, directly fly.
Imogen. [reads] 'He is one of the noblest note, to whose
  kindnesses I am most infinitely tied. Reflect upon him
  accordingly, as you value your trust.

                                 Leonatus.' 25

  So far I read aloud.
  But even the very middle of my heart
  Is warmed by th' rest and takes it thankfully.
  You are as welcome, worthy sir, as I
  Have words to bid you, and shall find it so   30
  In all that I can do.
Iachimo.   Thanks, fairest lady.
  What, are men mad? Hath nature given them eyes
  To see this vaulted arch and the rich crop

---

11 *Change you* i.e. change your expression; I have good news   15 *out of
door* visible   17 *Arabian bird* mythical phoenix (only one existed at a time;
hence, unique)   20 *Parthian* mounted archer who fired backwards while in
flight   22 *note* distinction   23 *Reflect upon* welcome   33 *crop* harvest

Of sea and land, which can distinguish 'twixt
35 The fiery orbs above and the twinned stones
Upon the numbered beach, and can we not
Partition make with spectacles so precious
'Twixt fair and foul?

Imogen.   What makes your admiration?

Iachimo. It cannot be i' th' eye, for apes and monkeys,
40 'Twixt two such shes, would chatter this way and
Contemn with mows the other; nor i' th' judgment,
For idiots, in this case of favor, would
Be wisely definite; nor i' th' appetite —
Sluttery, to such neat excellence opposed,
45 Should make desire vomit emptiness,
Not so allured to feed.

Imogen. What is the matter, trow?

Iachimo.   The cloyèd will —
That satiate yet unsatisfied desire, that tub
Both filled and running — ravening first the lamb,
Longs after for the garbage.

50 Imogen.   What, dear sir,
Thus raps you? Are you well?

Iachimo.   Thanks, madam, well.
[To Pisanio] Beseech you, sir, desire
My man's abode where I did leave him.
He's strange and peevish.

---

35 *twinned* exactly alike   36 *numbered* (with) numerous (stones)   37 *Partition* distinction   *spectacles* eyes   38 *admiration* wonder   40 *chatter this way* speak (i.e. give approval) for this one (Imogen)   41 *mows* grimaces   42 *case of favor* question of beauty   43 *Be wisely definite* make a wise decision   *appetite* physical desire   44 *neat* elegant   45 *desire* lust   *vomit emptiness* vomit though not fed   46 *so allured* attracted by this (i.e. by 'sluttery,' I. 44)   47 *trow* I wonder   *will* sexual desire   49 *ravening* feeding voraciously on   51 *raps* carries away   53 *man's abode* man to await   54 *strange* a stranger   *peevish* easily distressed

Pisanio.   I was going, sir,
　To give him welcome.   *Exit.* 55
Imogen. Continues well my lord? His health, beseech you?
Iachimo. Well, madam.
Imogen. Is he disposed to mirth? I hope he is.
Iachimo. Exceeding pleasant; none a stranger there
　So merry and so gamesome. He is called   60
　The Briton reveller.
Imogen.   When he was here
　He did incline to sadness, and ofttimes
　Not knowing why.
Iachimo.   I never saw him sad.
　There is a Frenchman his companion, one
　An eminent monsieur that, it seems, much loves   65
　A Gallian girl at home. He furnaces
　The thick sighs from him, whiles the jolly Briton —
　Your lord, I mean — laughs from's free lungs, cries 'O,
　Can my sides hold to think that man who knows
　By history, report, or his own proof   70
　What woman is, yea, what she cannot choose
　But must be, will 's free hours languish for
　Assurèd bondage?'
Imogen.   Will my lord say so?
Iachimo. Ay, madam, with his eyes in flood with laughter.
　It is a recreation to be by   75
　And hear him mock the Frenchman. But heavens know
　Some men are much to blame.
Imogen.   Not he, I hope.
Iachimo. Not he — but yet heaven's bounty towards him
　　might

62 *sadness* seriousness   66 *Gallian* French   *furnaces* blows forth like a
furnace   67 *thick* close together   72 *languish* give up to languishing
78 *bounty* i.e. in bestowing upon him his own qualities, and Imogen

Be used more thankfully. In himself 'tis much;
80 In you, which I account his, beyond all talents.
Whilst I am bound to wonder, I am bound
To pity too.

Imogen.   What do you pity, sir?

Iachimo. Two creatures heartily.

Imogen.   Am I one, sir?
You look on me. What wrack discern you in me
Deserves your pity?

85 *Iachimo.*   Lamentable! What,
To hide me from the radiant sun and solace
I' th' dungeon by a snuff!

Imogen.   I pray you, sir,
Deliver with more openness your answers
To my demands. Why do you pity me?

90 *Iachimo.* That others do,
I was about to say, enjoy your — but
It is an office of the gods to venge it,
Not mine to speak on't.

Imogen.   You do seem to know
Something of me or what concerns me. Pray you,
95 Since doubting things go ill often hurts more
Than to be sure they do — for certainties
Either are past remedies, or, timely knowing,
The remedy then born — discover to me
What both you spur and stop.

Iachimo.   Had I this cheek
100 To bathe my lips upon; this hand, whose touch,
Whose every touch, would force the feeler's soul

79 *'tis* i.e. heaven's bounty is 80 *talents* his own qualities (?) wealth (?)
84 *wrack* wreck, disaster 86 *solace* find pleasure 87 *snuff* partly con-
sumed candlewick 92 *office* duty 95 *doubting* fearing 97 *timely knowing* if one knows in time 98 *then* is then *discover* reveal 99 *spur and
stop* prod on (toward disclosure) and stop

To th' oath of loyalty; this object, which
Takes prisoner the wild motion of mine eye,
Fixing it only here; should I, damned then,
Slaver with lips as common as the stairs   105
That mount the Capitol; join gripes with hands
Made hard with hourly falsehood (falsehood, as
With labor); then by-peeping in an eye
Base and illustrious as the smoky light
That's fed with stinking tallow — it were fit   110
That all the plagues of hell should at one time
Encounter such revolt.
Imogen.   My lord, I fear,
Has forgot Britain.
Iachimo.   And himself. Not I
Inclined to this intelligence pronounce
The beggary of his change, but 'tis your graces   115
That from my mutest conscience to my tongue
Charms this report out.
Imogen.   Let me hear no more.
Iachimo. O dearest soul, your cause doth strike my heart
With pity that doth make me sick. A lady
So fair, and fastened to an empery   120
Would make the great'st king double, to be partnered
With tomboys hired with that self exhibition
Which your own coffers yield; with diseased ventures
That play with all infirmities for gold

107–8 *as With* as if made hard by   108 *by-peeping* looking sidelong   109 *il-lustrious* (for *illustrous,* not lustrous)   112 *Encounter such revolt* come upon
(as a punishment) such inconstancy   113–14 *Not . . . pronounce* though not
inclined to give this news, I report   115 *beggary* meanness, cheapness
116 *mutest conscience* most silent knowledge   120–21 *empery Would* empire
which would   121–22 *partnered With tomboys* treated the same as whores
122 *that self exhibition* the very allowance money   123 *ventures* traders (?)
adventuresses (?)   124 *play* gamble, toy

125 Which rottenness can lend nature; such boiled stuff
    As well might poison poison! Be revenged,
    Or she that bore you was no queen, and you
    Recoil from your great stock.

Imogen.   Revenged?
    How should I be revenged? If this be true —
130 As I have such a heart that both mine ears
    Must not in haste abuse — if it be true,
    How should I be revenged?

Iachimo.   Should he make me
    Live like Diana's priest betwixt cold sheets,
    Whiles he is vaulting variable ramps,
135 In your despite, upon your purse? Revenge it.
    I dedicate myself to your sweet pleasure,
    More noble than that runagate to your bed,
    And will continue fast to your affection,
    Still close as sure.

Imogen.   What ho, Pisanio!
140 *Iachimo.* Let me my service tender on your lips.

Imogen. Away, I do condemn mine ears that have
    So long attended thee. If thou wert honorable,
    Thou wouldst have told this tale for virtue, not
    For such an end thou seek'st, as base as strange.
145 Thou wrong'st a gentleman who is as far
    From thy report as thou from honor, and
    Solicit'st here a lady that disdains
    Thee and the devil alike. What ho, Pisanio!
    The King my father shall be made acquainted
150 Of thy assault. If he shall think it fit

125 *Which* i.e. infirmities *boiled stuff* i.e. women treated for veneral disease
by sweating 128 *Recoil . . . stock* fall away from (what is natural to) your
royal heredity 134 *variable ramps* various whores 137 *runagate to* truant
from 138 *fast* firm 139 *close* secret 142 *attended* listened to

A saucy stranger in his court to mart
As in a Romish stew and to expound
His beastly mind to us, he hath a court
He little cares for and a daughter who
He not respects at all. What ho, Pisanio!   155
Iachimo. O happy Leonatus! I may say
The credit that thy lady hath of thee
Deserves thy trust, and thy most perfect goodness
Her assured credit. Blessèd live you long,
A lady to the worthiest sir that ever   160
Country called his, and you his mistress, only
For the most worthiest fit. Give me your pardon.
I have spoke this to know if your affiance
Were deeply rooted, and shall make your lord
That which he is, new o'er; and he is one   165
The truest mannered, such a holy witch
That he enchants societies into him.
Half all men's hearts are his.
Imogen.   You make amends.
Iachimo. He sits 'mongst men like a descended god.
He hath a kind of honor sets him off   170
More than a mortal seeming. Be not angry,
Most mighty Princess, that I have adventured
To try your taking of a false report, which hath
Honored with confirmation your great judgment
In the election of a sir so rare,   175
Which you know cannot err. The love I bear him

151 *saucy* impudent   *to mart* should bargain   152 *stew* brothel   157 *credit
... of* faith ... in   158 *goodness* integrity (*deserves*)   161 *called his* called
its own   163 *affiance* loyalty   165 *new o'er* all over again (i.e. doubly so)
one above all; uniquely   166 *truest mannered* most honestly behaved   *witch*
charmer   167 *societies* social groups   *into* to   171 *mortal seeming* human
appearance   173 *try your taking* test your reception   175 *election* choice
176 *Which* i.e. who

63

Made me to fan you thus, but the gods made you,
Unlike all others, chaffless. Pray your pardon.
Imogen. All's well, sir. Take my pow'r i' th' court for
        yours.
180 *Iachimo.* My humble thanks. I had almost forgot
T' entreat your Grace but in a small request,
And yet of moment too, for it concerns
Your lord, myself, and other noble friends
Are partners in the business.
Imogen.   Pray what is't?
185 *Iachimo.* Some dozen Romans of us and your lord —
The best feather of our wing — have mingled sums
To buy a present for the Emperor;
Which I, the factor for the rest, have done
In France. 'Tis plate of rare device and jewels
190 Of rich and exquisite form, their values great,
And I am something curious, being strange,
To have them in safe stowage. May it please you
To take them in protection?
Imogen.   Willingly;
And pawn mine honor for their safety. Since
195 My lord hath interest in them, I will keep them
In my bedchamber.
Iachimo.   They are in a trunk
Attended by my men. I will make bold
To send them to you, only for this night.
I must aboard to-morrow.
Imogen.   O, no, no.
200 *Iachimo.* Yes, I beseech, or I shall short my word
By length'ning my return. From Gallia

177 *fan* winnow, i.e. test   178 *chaffless* faultless   182 *moment* importance
188 *factor* agent   191 *curious* anxious   *strange* foreign   200 *short* not
live up to

64

I crossed the seas on purpose and on promise
To see your Grace.
Imogen.   I thank you for your pains.
But not away to-morrow!
Iachimo.   O, I must, madam.
Therefore I shall beseech you, if you please   205
To greet your lord with writing, do't to-night.
I have outstood my time, which is material
To th' tender of our present.
Imogen.   I will write.
Send your trunk to me; it shall safe be kept
And truly yielded you. You're very welcome.   *Exeunt.* 210

Enter Cloten and the two Lords.   II, i

Cloten. Was there ever man had such luck? When I kissed
the jack upon an upcast, to be hit away! I had a hundred
pound on't. And then a whoreson jackanapes must take
me up for swearing, as if I borrowed mine oaths of him
and might not spend them at my pleasure.   5
1. Lord. What got he by that? You have broke his pate
with your bowl.
2. Lord. [*aside*] If his wit had been like him that broke it,
it would have run all out.
Cloten. When a gentleman is disposed to swear, it is not 10
for any standers-by to curtail his oaths. Ha?
2. Lord. No, my lord; [*aside*] nor crop the ears of them.

207 *outstood* outstayed   208 *tender* giving   II, i, 1–2 *kissed the jack*
touched the target (in game of bowls)   2 *upcast* throw (?) chance (?)
3 *whoreson jackanapes* (terms of abuse)   3–4 *take me up* take me to task
11 *curtail* cut down

65

Cloten. Whoreson dog, I gave him satisfaction! Would he had been one of my rank.

15 *2. Lord. [aside]* To have smelled like a fool.

Cloten. I am not vexed more at anything in th' earth. A pox on't! I had rather not be so noble as I am. They dare not fight with me because of the Queen my mother. Every jack-slave hath his bellyful of fighting, and I must
20 go up and down like a cock that nobody can match.

2. Lord. [aside] You are cock and capon too, and you crow cock with your comb on.

Cloten. Sayest thou?

2. Lord. It is not fit your lordship should undertake every
25 companion that you give offense to.

Cloten. No, I know that, but it is fit I should commit offense to my inferiors.

2. Lord. Ay, it is fit for your lordship only.

Cloten. Why, so I say.

30 *1. Lord.* Did you hear of a stranger that's come to court to-night?

Cloten. A stranger, and I not know on't?

2. Lord. [aside] He's a strange fellow himself, and knows it not.

35 *1. Lord.* There's an Italian come, and, 'tis thought, one of Leonatus' friends.

Cloten. Leonatus? A banished rascal, and he's another, whatsoever he be. Who told you of this stranger?

1. Lord. One of your lordship's pages.

40 *Cloten.* Is it fit I went to look upon him? Is there no derogation in't?

15 *smelled* (pun on *rank* in l. 14)   17 *pox* venereal disease (standard oath)
19 *jack-slave* lower-class person   21–22 *capon . . . on* (puns on meanings 'castration,' 'idiot,' 'coxcomb')   24 *undertake* 'take on'   25 *companion* fellow (term of contempt)   26–27 *commit offense* attack (with excretory pun)
40–41 *derogation* loss of dignity

2. Lord. You cannot derogate, my lord.

Cloten. Not easily, I think.

2. Lord. [aside] You are a fool granted; therefore your
    issues, being foolish, do not derogate.   45

Cloten. Come, I'll go see this Italian. What I have lost
    to-day at bowls I'll win to-night of him. Come, go.

2. Lord. I'll attend your lordship.

                  Exit [Cloten with First Lord].

    That such a crafty devil as is his mother
    Should yield the world this ass! A woman that   50
    Bears all down with her brain, and this her son
    Cannot take two from twenty, for his heart,
    And leave eighteen. Alas, poor princess,
    Thou divine Imogen, what thou endur'st,
    Betwixt a father by thy stepdame governed,   55
    A mother hourly coining plots, a wooer
    More hateful than the foul expulsion is
    Of thy dear husband, than that horrid act
    Of the divorce he'ld make. The heavens hold firm
    The walls of thy dear honor, keep unshaked   60
    That temple, thy fair mind, that thou mayst stand,
    T' enjoy thy banished lord and this great land!   *Exit.*

    Enter Imogen in her bed, and a Lady [attending].   II, ii

Imogen. Who's there? My woman Helen?

Lady.   Please you, madam.

Imogen. What hour is it?

Lady.   Almost midnight, madam.

---

42 *cannot derogate* i.e. have no dignity to lose 45 *issues* acts 51 *Bears all
down* triumphs over everything 52 *for his heart* for the life of him

Imogen. I have read three hours then. Mine eyes are weak.
     Fold down the leaf where I have left. To bed.
5   Take not away the taper, leave it burning;
     And if thou canst awake by four o' th' clock,
     I prithee call me. Sleep hath seized me wholly.

                             [Exit Lady.]

     To your protection I commend me, gods.
     From fairies and the tempters of the night
10   Guard me, beseech ye!

                Sleeps. Iachimo [comes] from the trunk.

Iachimo. The crickets sing, and man's o'erlabored sense
     Repairs itself by rest. Our Tarquin thus
     Did softly press the rushes ere he wakened
     The chastity he wounded. Cytherea,
15   How bravely thou becom'st thy bed, fresh lily,
     And whiter than the sheets! That I might touch!
     But kiss, one kiss! Rubies unparagoned,
     How dearly they do't! 'Tis her breathing that
     Perfumes the chamber thus. The flame o' th' taper
20   Bows toward her and would underpeep her lids
     To see th' enclosèd lights, now canopied
     Under these windows, white and azure-laced
     With blue of heaven's own tinct. But my design:
     To note the chamber. I will write all down:
25   Such and such pictures; there the window; such
     Th' adornment of her bed; the arras, figures,
     Why, such and such; and the contents o' th' story.
     Ah, but some natural notes about her body

II, ii, 9 *fairies* i.e. evil fairies   11 *o'erlabored* overworked, worn out
12 *Our Tarquin* Roman who raped Lucretia   13 *rushes* floor coverings
(Elizabethan)   14 *Cytherea* Venus   15 *bravely* finely   *lily* (emblem of chastity)   18 *they do't* i.e. her lips (rubies) kiss each other   20 *underpeep* peep
under   22 *windows* eyelids   *azure-laced* i.e. with blue veins   23 *tinct* hue
26 *arras* tapestry   27 *story* room (?) design on arras (?)   28 *notes* marks

Above ten thousand meaner movables
Would testify, t' enrich mine inventory. 30
O sleep, thou ape of death, lie dull upon her.
And be her sense but as a monument,
Thus in a chapel lying. Come off, come off —

[Takes off her bracelet.]

As slippery as the Gordian knot was hard.
'Tis mine, and this will witness outwardly, 35
As strongly as the conscience does within,
To th' madding of her lord. On her left breast
A mole cinque-spotted, like the crimson drops
I' th' bottom of a cowslip. Here's a voucher
Stronger than ever law could make. This secret 40
Will force him think I have picked the lock and ta'en
The treasure of her honor. No more. To what end?
Why should I write this down that's riveted,
Screwed to my memory? She hath been reading late
The tale of Tereus. Here the leaf's turned down 45
Where Philomel gave up. I have enough.
To th' trunk again, and shut the spring of it.
Swift, swift, you dragons of the night, that dawning
May bare the raven's eye. I lodge in fear.
Though this a heavenly angel, hell is here. *Clock strikes.* 50
One, two, three. Time, time! *Exit [into the trunk].*

---

29 *meaner movables* less important furnishings 31 *dull* heavy 32 *monument* i.e. sculptured human form lying horizontally on a tomb 34 *Gordian knot* intricate knot tied by Gordius, Phrygian king, and cut by Alexander the Great with his sword 36 *conscience* knowledge or consciousness (of Posthumus) 37 *madding* maddening 38 *cinque-spotted* with five spots 39 *voucher* evidence 40 *secret* intimate fact 45 *Tereus* Thracian king who raped his sister-in-law Philomela and cut out her tongue 49 *bare . . . eye* (the raven was believed to wake early)

Enter Cloten and Lords.

1. Lord. Your lordship is the most patient man in loss, the
most coldest that ever turned up ace.

Cloten. It would make any man cold to lose.

1. Lord. But not every man patient after the noble temper
5   of your lordship. You are most hot and furious when you
win.

Cloten. Winning will put any man into courage. If I could
get this foolish Imogen, I should have gold enough. It's
almost morning, is't not?

10 *1. Lord.* Day, my lord.

Cloten. I would this music would come. I am advised to
give her music a-mornings; they say it will penetrate.

Enter Musicians.

Come on, tune. If you can penetrate her with your fin-
gering, so; we'll try with tongue too. If none will do,
15   let her remain, but I'll never give o'er. First, a very excellent good-conceited thing; after, a wonderful sweet air
with admirable rich words to it – and then let her
consider.

Song.

Hark, hark, the lark at heaven's gate
sings,
20   And Phoebus gins arise,
His steeds to water at those springs
On chaliced flowers that lies;

II, iii, 2 *coldest* coolest, calmest   *turned up ace* made the lowest dice throw
(with pun on *ass*)   3 *cold* depressed   12, 13 *penetrate* affect emotionally
(with sexual innuendo)   14 *so* fine   15 *give o'er* give up   16 *good-
conceited* well-wrought   20 *Phoebus* Apollo, as the sun   *gins* begins to

And winking Mary-buds begin
To ope their golden eyes.
With every thing that pretty is,   25
My lady sweet, arise,
Arise, arise!

Cloten. So, get you gone. If this penetrate, I will consider
your music the better; if it do not, it is a vice in her ears
which horsehairs and calves' guts, nor the voice of un- 30
paved eunuch to boot, can never amend.

[Exeunt Musicians.]

Enter Cymbeline and Queen.

2. Lord. Here comes the King.

Cloten. I am glad I was up so late, for that's the reason I
was up so early. He cannot choose but take this service I
have done fatherly. Good morrow to your Majesty and 35
to my gracious mother.

Cymbeline. Attend you here the door of our stern daughter?
Will she not forth?

Cloten. I have assailed her with musics, but she vouchsafes
no notice.   40

Cymbeline. The exile of her minion is too new;
She hath not yet forgot him. Some more time
Must wear the print of his remembrance on't,
And then she's yours.

Queen.   You are most bound to th' King,
Who lets go by no vantages that may   45
Prefer you to his daughter. Frame yourself

23 *winking* closed *Mary-buds* marigold buds 28 *consider* recompense
29 *vice* flaw 30 *horsehairs* bowstrings   *calves' guts* fiddle strings
30-31 *unpaved* without stones (i.e. castrated) 35 *fatherly* as a father
(modifies *take*) 37 *Attend* wait at 41 *minion* darling 45 *vantages*
occasions 46 *Prefer* recommend *Frame* prepare

71

To orderly solicits, and be friended
With aptness of the season. Make denials
Increase your services. So seem as if
50 You were inspired to do those duties which
You tender to her; that you in all obey her,
Save when command to your dismission tends,
And therein you are senseless.
Cloten.   Senseless? Not so.

[Enter a Messenger.]

Messenger. So like you, sir, ambassadors from Rome.
The one is Caius Lucius.
55 *Cymbeline.*   A worthy fellow,
Albeit he comes on angry purpose now.
But that's no fault of his. We must receive him
According to the honor of his sender,
And towards himself, his goodness forespent on us,
60 We must extend our notice. Our dear son,
When you have given good morning to your mistress,
Attend the Queen and us. We shall have need
T' employ you towards this Roman. Come, our queen.
                              Exeunt [all but Cloten].
Cloten. If she be up, I'll speak with her; if not,
65 Let her lie still and dream. *[Knocks.]* By your leave, ho!
I know her women are about her. What
If I do line one of their hands? 'Tis gold
Which buys admittance — oft it doth — yea, and makes
Diana's rangers false themselves, yield up

47 *solicits* approaches, importunings 47–48 *be ... season* make good
use of appropriate times 48 *denials* rejections (by her) 52 *dismission*
dismissal 53 *are senseless* are not to understand (or obey) 54 *So like you*
if you please 59 *his ... us* because of his earlier goodness to us 67 *line* i.e.
with money 69 *rangers* gamekeepers (i.e. attendant nymphs, vowed to
chastity) *false* turn false

72

Their deer to th' stand o' th' stealer; and 'tis gold   70
Which makes the true man killed and saves the thief,
Nay, sometime hangs both thief and true man. What
Can it not do and undo? I will make
One of her women lawyer to me, for
I yet not understand the case myself.   75
By your leave.   *Knocks.*

Enter a Lady.

Lady. Who's there that knocks?
Cloten.   A gentleman.
Lady.   No more?
Cloten. Yes, and a gentlewoman's son.
Lady.   That's more
  Than some whose tailors are as dear as yours
  Can justly boast of. What's your lordship's pleasure?   80
Cloten. Your lady's person. Is she ready?
Lady.   Ay,
  To keep her chamber.
Cloten.   There is gold for you.
  Sell me your good report.
Lady. How? My good name? Or to report of you
  What I shall think is good? The Princess!   85

Enter Imogen.

Cloten. Good morrow, fairest sister. Your sweet hand.
                                          [Exit Lady.]
Imogen. Good morrow, sir. You lay out too much pains
  For purchasing but trouble. The thanks I give
  Is telling you that I am poor of thanks
  And scarce can spare them.

70 *stand* blind (hunter's station; with sexual innuendo)   75 *understand the case* know how to carry on the suit   81 *ready* dressed   87 *lay out* expend

73

90 *Cloten.*   Still I swear I love you.
   Imogen. If you but said so, 'twere as deep with me.
   If you swear still, your recompense is still
   That I regard it not.
   Cloten.   This is no answer.
   Imogen. But that you shall not say I yield being silent,
95 I would not speak. I pray you spare me. Faith,
   I shall unfold equal discourtesy
   To your best kindness. One of your great knowing
   Should learn, being taught, forbearance.
   Cloten. To leave you in your madness, 'twere my sin.
100 I will not.
   Imogen. Fools are not mad folks.
   Cloten.   Do you call me fool?
   Imogen. As I am mad, I do.
   If you'll be patient, I'll no more be mad;
   That cures us both. I am much sorry, sir,
105 You put me to forget a lady's manners
   By being so verbal; and learn now for all
   That I, which know my heart, do here pronounce
   By th' very truth of it, I care not for you,
   And am so near the lack of charity
110 To accuse myself I hate you — which I had rather
   You felt than make't my boast.
   Cloten.   You sin against
   Obedience, which you owe your father. For
   The contract you pretend with that base wretch,
   One bred of alms and fostered with cold dishes,

---

91 *deep* effective   92 *still* continually   94 *But that* in order that   96 *unfold* show   97 *knowing* knowledge (ironic)   106 *verbal* talkative, i.e. Cloten (?) outspoken, i.e. Imogen (?)   110 *To ... hate* that I must accuse myself of hating   112 *For* as for   113 *contract* i.e. of marriage *pretend* offer as an excuse (for not having me)

With scraps o' th' court—it is no contract, none.   115
And though it be allowed in meaner parties—
Yet who than he more mean?—to knit their souls,
On whom there is no more dependency
But brats and beggary, in self-figured knot;
Yet you are curbed from that enlargement by   120
The consequence o' th' crown, and must not foil
The precious note of it with a base slave,
A hilding for a livery, a squire's cloth,
A pantler—not so eminent.
Imogen.   Profane fellow!
Wert thou the son of Jupiter, and no more   125
But what thou art besides, thou wert too base
To be his groom. Thou wert dignified enough,
Even to the point of envy, if 'twere made
Comparative for your virtues to be styled
The under-hangman of his kingdom, and hated   130
For being preferred so well.
Cloten.   The south fog rot him!
Imogen. He never can meet more mischance than come
To be but named of thee. His meanest garment
That ever hath but clipped his body is dearer
In my respect than all the hairs above thee,   135
Were they all made such men. How now, Pisanio?

---

116 *meaner parties* lower-class people   118 *On . . . dependency* with no other consequence   119 *self-figured* self-arranged   120 *curbed . . . enlargement* restrained from that freedom   121 *consequence* what follows (from your inheritance) *foil* foul   122 *note* distinction   123 *hilding* good-for-nothing *for . . . cloth* suited for servant's attire   124 *pantler* pantry man *not* not even 127 *dignified* given honor   128–30 *if . . . kingdom* if, according to the virtue of each of you, you were made under-hangman and he king   131 *south fog* south wind, supposedly damp and unhealthful   133 *of* by   134 *clipped* embraced   135 *respect* regard   136 *How now* (Imogen suddenly notices that the bracelet is gone)

Enter Pisanio.

Cloten. 'His garment'? Now the devil –
Imogen. To Dorothy my woman hie thee presently.
Cloten. 'His garment'?
Imogen.   I am sprited with a fool,
140   Frighted, and ang'red worse. Go bid my woman
Search for a jewel that too casually
Hath left mine arm. It was thy master's. Shrew me
If I would lose it for a revenue
Of any king's in Europe. I do think
145   I saw't this morning; confident I am
Last night 'twas on mine arm; I kissed it.
I hope it be not gone to tell my lord
That I kiss aught but he.
Pisanio.   'Twill not be lost.
Imogen. I hope so. Go and search.   *[Exit Pisanio.]*
Cloten.   You have abused me.
'His meanest garment'?
150   *Imogen.*   Ay, I said so, sir.
If you will make't an action, call witness to't.
Cloten. I will inform your father.
Imogen.   Your mother too.
She's my good lady and will conceive, I hope,
But the worst of me. So I leave you, sir,
To th' worst of discontent.   *Exit.*
155   *Cloten.*   I'll be revenged.
'His meanest garment'? Well.   *Exit.*

139 *sprited* haunted   142 *Shrew* curse (mild, polite oath; here used emphatically)   149 *so* i.e. not   151 *action* lawsuit   153 *conceive* think, believe

Enter Posthumus and Philario.

Posthumus. Fear it not, sir. I would I were so sure
   To win the King as I am bold her honor
   Will remain hers.
Philario.   What means do you make to him?
Posthumus. Not any, but abide the change of time,
   Quake in the present winter's state, and wish   5
   That warmer days would come. In these feared hopes
   I barely gratify your love; they failing,
   I must die much your debtor.
Philario. Your very goodness and your company
   O'erpays all I can do. By this, your king   10
   Hath heard of great Augustus; Caius Lucius
   Will do's commission throughly. And I think
   He'll grant the tribute, send th' arrearages,
   Or look upon our Romans, whose remembrance
   Is yet fresh in their grief.
Posthumus.   I do believe,   15
   Statist though I am none, nor like to be,
   That this will prove a war; and you shall hear
   The legion now in Gallia sooner landed
   In our not-fearing Britain than have tidings
   Of any penny tribute paid. Our countrymen   20
   Are men more ordered than when Julius Caesar
   Smiled at their lack of skill but found their courage
   Worthy his frowning at. Their discipline,
   Now mingled with their courages, will make known

II, iv, 2 *bold* certain   3 *means* approaches   5 *winter's* i.e. bitter, outcast
6 *feared* fear-laden   7 *gratify* repay   10 *this* now   13 *He* Cymbeline
arrearages overdue payments of tribute   14 *Or* or else (?) before, rather
than (?)   15 *their* the Britons' (as caused by the Romans)   16 *Statist* states-
man   17 *prove* result in, turn out to be   21 *ordered* disciplined

25   To their approvers they are people such
      That mend upon the world.

Enter Iachimo.

Philario.   See, Iachimo!
Posthumus. The swiftest harts have posted you by land,
      And winds of all the corners kissed your sails
      To make your vessel nimble.
Philario.   Welcome, sir.
30 *Posthumus.* I hope the briefness of your answer made
      The speediness of your return.
Iachimo.   Your lady
      Is one of the fairest that I have looked upon.
Posthumus. And therewithal the best, or let her beauty
      Look through a casement to allure false hearts
      And be false with them.
35 *Iachimo.*   Here are letters for you.
Posthumus. Their tenor good, I trust.
Iachimo.   'Tis very like.
Philario. Was Caius Lucius in the Briton court
      When you were there?
Iachimo.   He was expected then,
      But not approached.
Posthumus.   All is well yet.
40   Sparkles this stone as it was wont, or is't not
      Too dull for your good wearing?
Iachimo.   If I have lost it,
      I should have lost the worth of it in gold.
      I'll make a journey twice as far t' enjoy
      A second night of such sweet shortness which

25 *approvers* those who test them   26 *mend upon* improve   27 *have posted*
must have sped   28 *corners* quarters   30 *your answer* (Imogen's) reply to
you   36 *like* likely

Was mine in Britain — for the ring is won. 45
Posthumus. The stone's too hard to come by.
Iachimo. `Not a whit,
Your lady being so easy.
Posthumus. Make not, sir,
Your loss your sport. I hope you know that we
Must not continue friends.
Iachimo. Good sir, we must,
If you keep covenant. Had I not brought 50
The knowledge of your mistress home, I grant
We were to question farther, but I now
Profess myself the winner of her honor,
Together with your ring, and not the wronger
Of her or you, having proceeded but 55
By both your wills.
Posthumus. If you can make't apparent
That you have tasted her in bed, my hand
And ring is yours. If not, the foul opinion
You had of her pure honor gains or loses
Your sword or mine, or masterless leave both 60
To who shall find them.
Iachimo. Sir, my circumstances,
Being so near the truth as I will make them,
Must first induce you to believe; whose strength
I will confirm with oath, which I doubt not
You'll give me leave to spare when you shall find 65
You need it not.
Posthumus. Proceed.
Iachimo. First, her bedchamber —

---

50 *keep covenant* hold to the bargain 51 *knowledge* i.e. sexual 52 *question*
dispute in a duel 60 *leave* let it leave (some editors emend to *leaves*)
61 *circumstances* circumstantial report 63 *whose* (antecedent is *circumstances*) 65 *spare* omit

Where I confess I slept not, but profess
Had that was well worth watching – it was hanged
With tapestry of silk and silver; the story
70 Proud Cleopatra, when she met her Roman
And Cydnus swelled above the banks, or for
The press of boats or pride: a piece of work
So bravely done, so rich, that it did strive
In workmanship and value; which I wondered
75 Could be so rarely and exactly wrought,
Since the true life on't was –

Posthumus.   This is true,
And this you might have heard of here, by me
Or by some other.

Iachimo.   More particulars
Must justify my knowledge.

Posthumus.   So they must,
Or do your honor injury.

80 *Iachimo.*   The chimney
Is south the chamber, and the chimney piece
Chaste Dian bathing. Never saw I figures
So likely to report themselves. The cutter
Was as another nature, dumb; outwent her,
Motion and breath left out.

85 *Posthumus.*   This is a thing
Which you might from relation likewise reap,
Being, as it is, much spoke of.

---

68 *watching* staying awake   71 *Cydnus* river where Antony and Cleopatra
met   71–72 *or . . . press* either because of the multitude   73 *bravely* finely
73–74 *did . . . value* it was a question whether form or content was better
79 *justify* prove   81 *south* on the south wall of *piece* art work   83 *likely*
to report able to identify *cutter* sculptor   84 *as . . . dumb* like nature (in
creative power) but unable to make a sculpture speak *outwent her* sur-
passed nature   85 *Motion . . . out* i.e. the sculpture cannot move or breathe
86 *from . . . reap* learn at second hand

Iachimo. The roof o' th' chamber
  With golden cherubins is fretted. Her andirons –
  I had forgot them – were two winking Cupids
  Of silver, each on one foot standing, nicely   90
  Depending on their brands.
Posthumus. This is her honor!
  Let it be granted you have seen all this – and praise
  Be given to your remembrance – the description
  Of what is in her chamber nothing saves
  The wager you have laid.
Iachimo. Then, if you can   95
                                       [Shows the bracelet.]
  Be pale, I beg but leave to air this jewel. See!
  And now 'tis up again. It must be married
  To that your diamond; I'll keep them.
Posthumus. Jove!
  Once more let me behold it. Is it that
  Which I left with her?
Iachimo. Sir, I thank her, that.   100
  She stripped it from her arm; I see her yet.
  Her pretty action did outsell her gift,
  And yet enriched it too. She gave it me and said
  She prized it once.
Posthumus. May be she plucked it off
  To send it me.
Iachimo. She writes so to you, doth she?   105
Posthumus. O, no, no, no, 'tis true. Here, take this too.
                                       [Gives the ring.]
  It is a basilisk unto mine eye,

88 *fretted* adorned by carvings   89 *winking* with eyes closed (i.e. blind)
91 *Depending . . . brands* leaning on their torches   94 *nothing saves* by no
means wins   96 *Be pale* stay unflushed (i.e. calm)   97 *up* put up (i.e. in
his pocket)   102 *outsell* exceed in value   107 *basilisk* mythical reptile,
believed to kill by look

  Kills me to look on't. Let there be no honor
  Where there is beauty; truth, where semblance; love,
110 Where there's another man. The vows of women
  Of no more bondage be to where they are made
  Than they are to their virtues, which is nothing.
  O, above measure false!
 Philario.   Have patience, sir,
  And take your ring again; 'tis not yet won.
115 It may be probable she lost it, or
  Who knows if one of her women, being corrupted,
  Hath stol'n it from her?
 Posthumus.   Very true,
  And so I hope he came by't. Back my ring;
  Render to me some corporal sign about her
120 More evident than this, for this was stol'n.
 Iachimo. By Jupiter, I had it from her arm.
 Posthumus. Hark you, he swears; by Jupiter he swears.
  'Tis true—nay, keep the ring—'tis true. I am sure
  She would not lose it. Her attendants are
125 All sworn and honorable. They induced to steal it?
  And by a stranger? No, he hath enjoyed her.
  The cognizance of her incontinency
  Is this. She hath bought the name of whore thus dearly.
  There, take thy hire, and all the fiends of hell
  Divide themselves between you!
130 *Philario.*   Sir, be patient.
  This is not strong enough to be believed
  Of one persuaded well of.
 Posthumus.   Never talk on't.

110–11 *The vows . . . made* let women's vows no more bind them to men
115 *probable* provable 118 *so* in this manner 120 *More evident* which is
better evidence 125 *sworn* bound (as if) by oath 127 *cognizance* identify-
ing mark 128 *this* i.e. the ring 129 *hire* winnings 132 *persuaded well of*
well thought of

She hath been colted by him.
Iachimo. If you seek
For further satisfying, under her breast—
Worthy the pressing—lies a mole, right proud   135
Of that most delicate lodging. By my life,
I kissed it, and it gave me present hunger
To feed again, though full. You do remember
This stain upon her?
Posthumus. Ay, and it doth confirm
Another stain, as big as hell can hold,   140
Were there no more but it.
Iachimo. Will you hear more?
Posthumus. Spare your arithmetic; never count the turns.
Once, and a million!
Iachimo. I'll be sworn.
Posthumus. No swearing.
If you will swear you have not done't, you lie,
And I will kill thee if thou dost deny   145
Thou'st made me cuckold.
Iachimo. I'll deny nothing.
Posthumus. O that I had her here, to tear her limb-meal!
I will go there and do't i' th' court, before
Her father. I'll do something. *Exit.*
Philario. Quite besides
The government of patience! You have won.   150
Let's follow him and pervert the present wrath
He hath against himself.
Iachimo. With all my heart. *Exeunt.*

---

133 *been colted by* had intercourse with   137 *present* immediate   139 *stain*
mark, discoloration   140 *stain* moral flaw   142 *turns* occasions, deviations
147 *limb-meal* limb from limb   149–50 *besides The government* beyond the
control   151 *pervert* turn aside

Enter Posthumus.

   Posthumus. Is there no way for men to be, but women
      Must be half-workers? We are all bastards,
      And that most venerable man which I
      Did call my father was I know not where
5   When I was stamped. Some coiner with his tools
      Made me a counterfeit; yet my mother seemed
      The Dian of that time. So doth my wife
      The nonpareil of this. O, vengeance, vengeance!
      Me of my lawful pleasure she restrained
10   And prayed me oft forbearance – did it with
      A pudency so rosy, the sweet view on't
      Might well have warmed old Saturn – that I thought her
      As chaste as unsunned snow. O, all the devils!
      This yellow Iachimo in an hour, was't not?
15   Or less? At first? Perchance he spoke not, but,
      Like a full-acorned boar, a German one,
      Cried 'O!' and mounted; found no opposition
      But what he looked for should oppose and she
      Should from encounter guard. Could I find out
20   The woman's part in me! For there's no motion
      That tends to vice in man but I affirm
      It is the woman's part. Be it lying, note it,
      The woman's; flattering, hers; deceiving, hers;
      Lust and rank thoughts, hers, hers; revenges, hers;
25   Ambitions, covetings, change of prides, disdain,
      Nice longing, slanders, mutability,

II, v, 1 *be* exist   2 *half-workers* i.e. in begetting   5 *stamped* minted (i.e. be-gotten)   8 *nonpareil* one without equal   11 *pudency* modesty   12 *Saturn* (this god was thought to be cold and gloomy; cf. 'saturnine')   14 *yellow* i.e. in complexion   15 *At first* immediately   16 *full-acorned* full of acorns *German* (allusion not clear)   20–21 *motion . . . to* impulse toward   25 *change of prides* series of vanities   26 *Nice* finicky or lascivious *mutability* fickleness

All faults that man may name, nay, that hell knows,
Why, hers, in part or all, but rather all.
For even to vice
They are not constant, but are changing still   30
One vice but of a minute old for one
Not half so old as that. I'll write against them,
Detest them, curse them. Yet 'tis greater skill
In a true hate to pray they have their will;
The very devils cannot plague them better.   *Exit.* 35

Enter in state Cymbeline, Queen, Cloten, and Lords at   III, i
one door, and at another, Caius Lucius and Attendants.

Cymbeline. Now say, what would Augustus Caesar with
    us?
Lucius. When Julius Caesar, whose remembrance yet
    Lives in men's eyes and will to ears and tongues
    Be theme and hearing ever, was in this Britain
    And conquered it, Cassibelan thine uncle,   5
    Famous in Caesar's praises no whit less
    Than in his feats deserving it, for him
    And his succession granted Rome a tribute,
    Yearly three thousand pounds, which by thee lately
    Is left untendered.
Queen.   And, to kill the marvel,   10
    Shall be so ever.
Cloten.   There be many Caesars
    Ere such another Julius. Britain's a world
    By itself, and we will nothing pay

III, i, 10 *kill the marvel* eliminate the surprise (i.e. when non-payment is
standard procedure)

For wearing our own noses.

Queen.   That opportunity
15 Which then they had to take from's, to resume
We have again. Remember, sir, my liege,
The kings your ancestors, together with
The natural bravery of your isle, which stands
As Neptune's park, ribbèd and palèd in
20 With rocks unscalable and roaring waters,
With sands that will not bear your enemies' boats
But suck them up to th' topmast. A kind of conquest
Caesar made here, but made not here his brag
Of 'Came and saw and overcame.' With shame,
25 The first that ever touched him, he was carried
From off our coast, twice beaten; and his shipping,
Poor ignorant baubles on our terrible seas,
Like eggshells moved upon their surges, cracked
As easily 'gainst our rocks. For joy whereof
30 The famed Cassibelan, who was once at point —
O giglet fortune! — to master Caesar's sword,
Made Lud's town with rejoicing fires bright
And Britons strut with courage.

Cloten. Come, there's no more tribute to be paid. Our
35 kingdom is stronger than it was at that time, and, as I
said, there is no moe such Caesars. Other of them may
have crook'd noses, but to owe such straight arms, none.

Cymbeline. Son, let your mother end.

Cloten. We have yet many among us can gripe as hard as
40 Cassibelan. I do not say I am one, but I have a hand.
Why tribute? Why should we pay tribute? If Caesar can

15 *resume* take back 19 *ribbèd* enclosed *palèd* fenced 21 *sands* i.e. quick-
sands 27 *ignorant* silly, inexperienced 30–31 *at point . . . to master* on the
point . . . of mastering 31 *giglet* wanton, promiscuous 32 *Lud's town*
London (after Lud, legendary king) 37 *crook'd* i.e. Roman (cf. l. 14)
owe own 39 *gripe* grip (in combat)

hide the sun from us with a blanket or put the moon in
his pocket, we will pay him tribute for light; else, sir, no
more tribute, pray you now.

Cymbeline. You must know,   45
  Till the injurious Romans did extort
  This tribute from us, we were free. Caesar's ambition,
  Which swelled so much that it did almost stretch
  The sides o' th' world, against all color here
  Did put the yoke upon's; which to shake off   50
  Becomes a warlike people, whom we reckon
  Ourselves to be, we do. Say then to Caesar,
  Our ancestor was that Mulmutius which
  Ordained our laws, whose use the sword of Caesar
  Hath too much mangled, whose repair and franchise   55
  Shall, by the power we hold, be our good deed,
  Though Rome be therefore angry. Mulmutius made our
        laws,
  Who was the first of Britain which did put
  His brows within a golden crown and called
  Himself a king.

Lucius.   I am sorry, Cymbeline,   60
  That I am to pronounce Augustus Caesar —
  Caesar, that hath moe kings his servants than
  Thyself domestic officers — thine enemy.
  Receive it from me then: war and confusion
  In Caesar's name pronounce I 'gainst thee. Look   65
  For fury not to be resisted. Thus defied,
  I thank thee for myself.

46 *injurious* insolent   49 *against all color* without any justifying pre-
text (with pun on *collar;* note *yoke* in l. 50)   52 *we do* i.e. shake off (some
editors begin the next sentence with 'we do')   53 *Mulmutius* earlier king,
told about in chronicles   55 *whose* (the antecedent is *laws*) *franchise* free
exercise   61 *pronounce* declare   62 *moe* more   *his* as his   64 *confusion* destruction

   Cymbeline.   Thou art welcome, Caius.
   Thy Caesar knighted me; my youth I spent
   Much under him; of him I gathered honor,
70 Which he to seek of me again, perforce,
   Behooves me keep at utterance. I am perfect
   That the Pannonians and Dalmatians for
   Their liberties are now in arms, a precedent
   Which not to read would show the Britons cold.
   So Caesar shall not find them.
75 *Lucius.*   Let proof speak.
   Cloten. His Majesty bids you welcome. Make pastime with
   us a day or two, or longer. If you seek us afterwards in
   other terms, you shall find us in our salt-water girdle; if
   you beat us out of it, it is yours. If you fall in the adven-
80 ture, our crows shall fare the better for you, and there's
   an end.
   Lucius. So, sir.
   Cymbeline. I know your master's pleasure, and he mine.
   All the remain is, welcome.   *Exeunt.*

III, ii   *Enter Pisanio, reading of a letter.*

   Pisanio. How? Of adultery? Wherefore write you not
   What monsters her accuse? Leonatus,
   O master, what a strange infection
   Is fall'n into thy ear! What false Italian,
5 As poisonous tongued as handed, hath prevailed

---

70 *he to seek* since he seeks it *perforce* of necessity 71 *keep at utterance* to
defend to the uttermost *perfect* well aware 72 *Pannonians and Dalmatians*
inhabitants of present-day Balkan regions 74 *cold* lacking spirit 75 *Let
proof speak* let the military test settle it 84 *the remain* that remains

On thy too ready hearing? Disloyal? No.
She's punished for her truth and undergoes,
More goddess-like than wife-like, such assaults
As would take in some virtue. O my master,
Thy mind to her is now as low as were   10
Thy fortunes. How? That I should murder her,
Upon the love and truth and vows which I
Have made to thy command? I her? Her blood?
If it be so to do good service, never
Let me be counted serviceable. How look I   15
That I should seem to lack humanity
So much as this fact comes to? *[Reads]* 'Do't! The letter
That I have sent her, by her own command
Shall give thee opportunity.' O damned paper,
Black as the ink that's on thee! Senseless bauble,   20
Art thou a fedary for this act, and look'st
So virgin-like without? Lo, here she comes.

Enter Imogen.

I am ignorant in what I am commanded.
Imogen. How now, Pisanio?
Pisanio. Madam, here is a letter from my lord.   25
Imogen. Who, thy lord? That is my lord Leonatus?
O, learn'd indeed were that astronomer
That knew the stars as I his characters;
He'ld lay the future open. You good gods,
Let what is here contained relish of love,   30
Of my lord's health, of his content — yet not
That we two are asunder; let that grieve him.

III, ii, 7 *truth* fidelity *undergoes* bears 9 *take in* conquer 10 *to* com-
pared with 17 *fact* deed 20 *Senseless bauble* inanimate trifle 21 *fedary
for* confederate in 23 *am ignorant* will pretend ignorance 27 *astronomer*
astrologer 28 *characters* handwriting 30 *relish* taste 31 *not* not content

Some griefs are med'cinable; that is one of them,
For it doth physic love — of his content
35 All but in that. Good wax, thy leave. Blest be
You bees that make these locks of counsel. Lovers
And men in dangerous bonds pray not alike;
Though forfeiters you cast in prison, yet
You clasp young Cupid's tables. Good news, gods!

[Reads.]

40   'Justice and your father's wrath, should he take me in
his dominion, could not be so cruel to me as you, O the
dearest of creatures, would even renew me with your
eyes. Take notice that I am in Cambria at Milford Haven.
What your own love will out of this advise you, follow.
45 So he wishes you all happiness that remains loyal to his
vow, and your increasing in love.

Leonatus Posthumus.'

O, for a horse with wings! Hear'st thou, Pisanio?
He is at Milford Haven. Read, and tell me
50 How far 'tis thither. If one of mean affairs
May plod it in a week, why may not I
Glide thither in a day? Then, true Pisanio,
Who long'st like me to see thy lord, who long'st —
O, let me bate — but not like me, yet long'st,
55 But in a fainter kind — O, not like me!
For mine's beyond beyond: say, and speak thick —

33 *are med'cinable* have medicinal value   34 *physic* medicate; increase the
strength of   35 *wax* i.e. in the seal of the letter   36 *locks of counsel* seals for
confidential matters   37 *in . . . bonds* under bonds imposing penalties
pray not alike i.e. lovers adore, bonded men hate, waxen seals   38 *forfeiters*
those who do not live up to bonds   39 *clasp . . . tables* fasten love letters
40 *take* capture   41–42 *as . . . renew* that you could not restore   43 *Cambria*
Wales   46 *increasing* (object of *wishes*)   50 *mean affairs* trivial business
54 *bate* abate, tone down (the statement)   56 *thick* fast

Love's counsellor should fill the bores of hearing,
To th' smothering of the sense — how far it is
To this same blessèd Milford. And by th' way
Tell me how Wales was made so happy as   60
T' inherit such a haven. But first of all,
How we may steal from hence, and for the gap
That we shall make in time from our hence-going
And our return, to excuse. But first, how get hence?
Why should excuse be born or ere begot?   65
We'll talk of that hereafter. Prithee speak,
How many score of miles may we well rid
'Twixt hour and hour?

Pisanio.   One score 'twixt sun and sun,
Madam, 's enough for you, and too much too.

Imogen. Why, one that rode to's execution, man,   70
Could never go so slow. I have heard of riding wagers
Where horses have been nimbler than the sands
That run i' th' clock's behalf. But this is fool'ry.
Go bid my woman feign a sickness, say
She'll home to her father; and provide me presently   75
A riding suit, no costlier than would fit
A franklin's housewife.

Pisanio.   Madam, you're best consider.

Imogen. I see before me, man. Nor here, nor here,
Nor what ensues, but have a fog in them
That I cannot look through. Away, I prithee;   80

---

57 *counsellor* helper *bores of hearing* ears 58 *To ... sense* and even over-
whelm the hearing 59 *by th' way* on the way 62–64 *for ... excuse* how to
account for the elapsed time, etc. 65 *or ere begot* i.e. before it is made necessary by what we do 67 *rid* get rid of, cover 71 *riding wagers* racing bets
73 *i' th' clock's behalf* i.e. in an hourglass 75 *home* go home *presently*
without delay 77 *franklin* freeholder (small land-owner) *you're best* you
had better 78 *before me* i.e. the road to Milford *Nor ... here* i.e. neither
to right nor to left 79 *what ensues* the eventual outcome

Do as I bid thee. There's no more to say.
Accessible is none but Milford way.   *Exeunt.*

III, iii   *Enter [from their cave] Belarius, Guiderius, and Arviragus.*

Belarius. A goodly day not to keep house with such
     Whose roof's as low as ours! Stoop, boys. This gate
     Instructs you how t' adore the heavens and bows you
     To a morning's holy office. The gates of monarchs
5   Are arched so high that giants may jet through
     And keep their impious turbans on without
     Good morrow to the sun. Hail, thou fair heaven!
     We house i' th' rock, yet use thee not so hardly
     As prouder livers do.
Guiderius.   Hail, heaven!
Arviragus.   Hail, heaven!
10 *Belarius.* Now for our mountain sport. Up to yond hill;
     Your legs are young. I'll tread these flats. Consider,
     When you above perceive me like a crow,
     That it is place which lessens and sets off,
     And you may then revolve what tales I have told you
15   Of courts, of princes, of the tricks in war.
     This service is not service, so being done,
     But being so allowed. To apprehend thus
     Draws us a profit from all things we see,
     And often, to our comfort, shall we find
20   The sharded beetle in a safer hold
     Than is the full-winged eagle. O, this life

III, iii, 1 *keep house* stay in   3 *bows you* makes you bow   4 *holy office* religious service   5 *jet* strut   8 *use* treat   *hardly* badly   9 *prouder livers* people who live more resplendently   13 *place* position   *sets off* embellishes   16 *This* any act of   17 *allowed* acknowledged   *To ... thus* to look at things in this way   20 *sharded* with scaly wing covers   *hold* stronghold

Is nobler than attending for a check,
Richer than doing nothing for a robe,
Prouder than rustling in unpaid-for silk:
Such gain the cap of him that makes him fine   25
Yet keeps his book uncrossed. No life to ours.
Guiderius. Out of your proof you speak. We poor unfledged
  Have never winged from view o' th' nest, nor know not
  What air 's from home. Haply this life is best
  If quiet life be best, sweeter to you   30
  That have a sharper known, well corresponding
  With your stiff age; but unto us it is
  A cell of ignorance, travelling abed,
  A prison, or a debtor that not dares
  To stride a limit.
Arviragus.   What should we speak of   35
  When we are old as you? When we shall hear
  The rain and wind beat dark December, how
  In this our pinching cave shall we discourse
  The freezing hours away? We have seen nothing.
  We are beastly: subtle as the fox for prey,   40
  Like warlike as the wolf for what we eat.
  Our valor is to chase what flies. Our cage
  We make a choir, as doth the prisoned bird,
  And sing our bondage freely.
Belarius.   How you speak!
  Did you but know the city's usuries   45
  And felt them knowingly; the art o' th' court,

22 *attending . . . check* doing service (at court) only to get a rebuke   23 *robe*
i.e. of office   25 *gain . . . fine* is respected by the elegant man   26 *keeps*
. . . uncrossed does not cross off (pay the debts in) his record-book (possibly,
tailor)   27 *proof* experience   29 *air 's* the air is like   *from* away from
Haply perhaps   33 *abed* i.e. in imagination   35 *stride a limit* cross a
boundary (and thus risk arrest)   38 *pinching* i.e. with cold   40 *beastly*
beast-like   41 *Like* as

As hard to leave as keep, whose top to climb
Is certain falling, or so slipp'ry that
The fear 's as bad as falling; the toil o' th' war,
50 A pain that only seems to seek out danger
I' th' name of fame and honor, which dies i' th' search
And hath as oft a sland'rous epitaph
As record of fair act; nay, many times
Doth ill deserve by doing well; what's worse,
55 Must curtsy at the censure. O boys, this story
The world may read in me. My body 's marked
With Roman swords, and my report was once
First with the best of note. Cymbeline loved me,
And when a soldier was the theme, my name
60 Was not far off. Then was I as a tree
Whose boughs did bend with fruit. But in one night
A storm or robbery, call it what you will,
Shook down my mellow hangings, nay, my leaves,
And left me bare to weather.

Guiderius.   Uncertain favor!

65 *Belarius.* My fault being nothing, as I have told you oft,
But that two villains, whose false oaths prevailed
Before my perfect honor, swore to Cymbeline
I was confederate with the Romans. So
Followed my banishment, and this twenty years
70 This rock and these demesnes have been my world,
Where I have lived at honest freedom, paid
More pious debts to heaven than in all
The fore-end of my time. But up to th' mountains!
This is not hunters' language. He that strikes

47 *keep* stay in   50 *pain* labor   51 *which* (the antecedent may be *pain* or *fame and honor*)   53 *fair act* fine deed   54 *deserve* earn, get   57 *report* reputation   58 *best of note* most distinguished   63 *hangings* fruit 66–67 *prevailed Before* had more weight than   70 *demesnes* regions 71 *at* in   73 *fore-end . . . time* early part of my life

The venison first shall be the lord o' th' feast;   75
To him the other two shall minister,
And we will fear no poison, which attends
In place of greater state. I'll meet you in the valleys.
                            Exeunt [Guiderius and Arviragus].
How hard it is to hide the sparks of nature!
These boys know little they are sons to th' King,   80
Nor Cymbeline dreams that they are alive.
They think they are mine, and though trained up thus
     meanly
I' th' cave wherein they bow, their thoughts do hit
The roofs of palaces, and nature prompts them
In simple and low things to prince it much   85
Beyond the trick of others. This Polydore,
The heir of Cymbeline and Britain, who
The King his father called Guiderius — Jove!
When on my three-foot stool I sit and tell
The warlike feats I have done, his spirits fly out   90
Into my story; say 'Thus mine enemy fell,
And thus I set my foot on's neck,' even then
The princely blood flows in his cheek, he sweats,
Strains his young nerves, and puts himself in posture
That acts my words. The younger brother Cadwal,   95
Once Arviragus, in as like a figure
Strikes life into my speech and shows much more
His own conceiving. Hark, the game is roused!
O Cymbeline, heaven and my conscience knows
Thou didst unjustly banish me; whereon,   100
At three and two years old, I stole these babes,

77 *attends* is to be expected   83-84 *do hit . . . palaces* i.e. are elevated, aspire
greatly   85 *prince* act like a prince   86 *trick* aptitude   90-91 *fly out Into*
(cf. 'empathize')   91 *say* (parallel with *tell* in l. 89)   94 *nerves* sinews
96 *in . . . figure* with an equally good acting out   98 *conceiving* interpretation   *roused* flushed

Thinking to bar thee of succession as
Thou reft'st me of my lands. Euriphile,
Thou wast their nurse; they took thee for their mother,
105 And every day do honor to her grave.
Myself, Belarius, that am Morgan called,
They take for natural father. The game is up.   *Exit.*

          Enter Pisanio and Imogen.

Imogen. Thou told'st me, when we came from horse, the place
  Was near at hand. Ne'er longed my mother so
To see me first as I have now. Pisanio, man,
Where is Posthumus? What is in thy mind
5 That makes thee stare thus? Wherefore breaks that sigh
From th' inward of thee? One but painted thus
Would be interpreted a thing perplexed
Beyond self-explication. Put thyself
Into a havior of less fear, ere wildness
10 Vanquish my staider senses. What's the matter?
Why tender'st thou that paper to me with
A look untender? If't be summer news,
Smile to't before; if winterly, thou need'st
But keep that count'nance still. My husband's hand?
15 That drug-damned Italy hath outcraftied him,
And he's at some hard point. Speak, man! Thy tongue
May take off some extremity, which to read

103 *reft'st* robbed 105 *her* i.e. Euriphile's 107 *game is up* (repeats l. 98)
III, iv, 1 *came from horse* dismounted 3 *have* i.e. longing to see Posthumus
7 *perplexed* troubled 9 *havior . . . fear* less frightening demeanor *wildness*
panic 10 *staider senses* more balanced feelings 12, 13 *summer, winterly*
good, bad 15 *drug-damned* cursed by the use of drugs *outcraftied* been
too crafty for 16 *hard point* (cf. 'tough spot') 17 *take . . . extremity* reduce
the extreme painfulness (of the news)

Would be even mortal to me.
Pisanio.   Please you read,
And you shall find me, wretched man, a thing
The most disdained of fortune.   20
Imogen. [reads] 'Thy mistress, Pisanio, hath played the
strumpet in my bed, the testimonies whereof lie bleeding
in me. I speak not out of weak surmises, but from proof
as strong as my grief and as certain as I expect my revenge.
That part thou, Pisanio, must act for me, if thy faith be   25
not tainted with the breach of hers. Let thine own hands
take away her life. I shall give thee opportunity at Mil-
ford Haven — she hath my letter for the purpose — where,
if thou fear to strike and to make me certain it is done,
thou art the pander to her dishonor and equally to me   30
disloyal.'
Pisanio. What shall I need to draw my sword? The paper
Hath cut her throat already. No, 'tis slander,
Whose edge is sharper than the sword, whose tongue
Outvenoms all the worms of Nile, whose breath   35
Rides on the posting winds and doth belie
All corners of the world. Kings, queens, and states,
Maids, matrons, nay, the secrets of the grave
This viperous slander enters. What cheer, madam?
Imogen. False to his bed? What is it to be false?   40
To lie in watch there and to think on him?
To weep 'twixt clock and clock? If sleep charge nature,
To break it with a fearful dream of him
And cry myself awake? That's false to's bed, is it?
Pisanio. Alas, good lady!   45

18 *mortal* fatal   26 *tainted* contaminated   35 *worms* serpents   36 *posting*
speeding   *belie* spread lies over   37 *states* people of national importance
41 *in watch* awake   42 *'twixt . . . clock* from hour to hour   *charge* burden
43 *fearful . . . him* dream involving fear for him

Imogen. I false? Thy conscience witness! Iachimo,
Thou didst accuse him of incontinency.
Thou then lookedst like a villain; now, methinks,
Thy favor 's good enough. Some jay of Italy,
50 Whose mother was her painting, hath betrayed him.
Poor I am stale, a garment out of fashion,
And, for I am richer than to hang by th' walls,
I must be ripped. To pieces with me! O,
Men's vows are women's traitors! All good seeming,
55 By thy revolt, O husband, shall be thought
Put on for villainy, not born where't grows,
But worn a bait for ladies.

Pisanio.   Good madam, hear me.

Imogen. True honest men, being heard like false Aeneas,
Were in his time thought false, and Sinon's weeping
60 Did scandal many a holy tear, took pity
From most true wretchedness. So thou, Posthumus,
Wilt lay the leaven on all proper men;
Goodly and gallant shall be false and perjured
From thy great fail. Come, fellow, be thou honest;
65 Do thou thy master's bidding. When thou seest him,
A little witness my obedience. Look,
I draw the sword myself. Take it, and hit
The innocent mansion of my love, my heart.
Fear not, 'tis empty of all things but grief.

46 *Thy* i.e. Posthumus's 49 *favor* countenance *jay* whore 50 *Whose
. . . painting* i.e. produced by painting, not by nature; false 52 *for . . . than*
since I'm too rich 54 *seeming* appearance 55 *By thy revolt* because of
thy turning away (infidelity) 56 *born* i.e. natural 58 *heard* i.e. heard to
speak *false Aeneas* (he deserted Dido) 59 *Sinon* (who won the confidence
of the Trojans by complaining of his treatment at the hands of his fellow
Greeks, and was thus able to persuade them to admit the wooden horse, in
which Greek warriors were concealed) 60 *scandal* discredit 62 *lay . . .
men* destroy confidence in honest men 63 *be* i.e. seem 64 *From . . . fail*
because of your falseness 66 *witness* testify to

Thy master is not there, who was indeed   70
The riches of it. Do his bidding, strike!
Thou mayst be valiant in a better cause,
But now thou seem'st a coward.
Pisanio.   Hence, vile instrument!
Thou shalt not damn my hand.
Imogen.   Why, I must die,
And if I do not by thy hand, thou art   75
No servant of thy master's. Against self-slaughter
There is a prohibition so divine
That cravens my weak hand. Come, here's my heart —
Something's afore't; soft, soft, we'll no defense —
Obedient as the scabbard. What is here?   80
The scriptures of the loyal Leonatus
All turned to heresy? Away, away,
Corrupters of my faith! You shall no more
Be stomachers to my heart. [*Takes his letters out of her
    bodice.*] Thus may poor fools
Believe false teachers. Though those that are betrayed   85
Do feel the treason sharply, yet the traitor
Stands in worse case of woe.
And thou, Posthumus, that didst set up
My disobedience 'gainst the King my father
And make me put into contempt the suits   90
Of princely fellows, shalt hereafter find
It is no act of common passage, but
A strain of rareness; and I grieve myself
To think, when thou shalt be disedged by her

78 *cravens* makes cowardly 79 *Something* i.e. Posthumus's letter, which she
speaks of as if it were armor 80 *Obedient* i.e. in receiving the sword
81 *scriptures* letter (with pun on 'Scriptures') 84 *stomachers* decorative
breast-coverings 87 *Stands . . . woe* is worse off 88 *set up* spur, push
92–93 *It . . . rareness* my choice was not an every-day occurrence but the result of a rare trait 94 *disedged* dulled (in sexual desire)

95   That now thou tirest on, how thy memory
        Will then be panged by me. Prithee dispatch,
        The lamb entreats the butcher. Where's thy knife?
        Thou art too slow to do thy master's bidding
        When I desire it too.

Pisanio.   O gracious lady,
100   Since I received command to do this business
        I have not slept one wink.

Imogen.   Do't, and to bed then.

Pisanio. I'll wake mine eyeballs out first.

Imogen.   Wherefore then
        Didst undertake it? Why hast thou abused
        So many miles with a pretense? This place?
105   Mine action and thine own? Our horses' labor?
        The time inviting thee? The perturbed court
        For my being absent? whereunto I never
        Purpose return. Why hast thou gone so far,
        To be unbent when thou hast ta'en thy stand,
        Th' elected deer before thee?

110 *Pisanio.*   But to win time
        To lose so bad employment, in the which
        I have considered of a course. Good lady,
        Hear me with patience.

Imogen.   Talk thy tongue weary, speak.
        I have heard I am a strumpet, and mine ear,
115   Therein false struck, can take no greater wound,
        Nor tent to bottom that. But speak.

Pisanio.   Then, madam,

---

95 *tirest on* devourest (like a bird of prey) 96 *panged* made miserable
102 *wake . . . out* stay awake until my eyeballs come out 103 *abused* made
bad use of 109 *unbent* i.e. not shooting (the figure is that of a bow)
110 *elected* chosen 111 *which* (the antecedent is *time*) 115 *take* receive
116 *tent . . . that* probe that (wound) to its depths

I thought you would not back again.

Imogen.   Most like,
Bringing me here to kill me.

Pisanio.   Not so, neither.
But if I were as wise as honest, then
My purpose would prove well. It cannot be   120
But that my master is abused. Some villain,
Ay, and singular in his art, hath done you both
This cursèd injury.

Imogen. Some Roman courtesan.

Pisanio.   No, on my life.
I'll give but notice you are dead, and send him   125
Some bloody sign of it, for 'tis commanded
I should do so. You shall be missed at court,
And that will well confirm it.

Imogen.   Why, good fellow,
What shall I do the while? Where bide? How live?
Or in my life what comfort when I am   130
Dead to my husband?

Pisanio.   If you'll back to th' court —

Imogen. No court, no father, nor no more ado
With that harsh, noble, simple nothing,
That Cloten, whose love suit hath been to me
As fearful as a siege.

Pisanio.   If not at court,   135
Then not in Britain must you bide.

Imogen.   Where then?
Hath Britain all the sun that shines? Day, night,
Are they not but in Britain? I' th' world's volume
Our Britain seems as of it, but not in't;

---

117 *back* go back   121 *abused* deceived   122 *singular* without equal
124 *No . . . life* (repeats his assertion of l. 118)   128 *it* i.e. your death
139 *of . . . in't* belonging to it but separated from it

140   In a great pool a swan's nest. Prithee think
       There's livers out of Britain.

Pisanio.   I am most glad
       You think of other place. Th' ambassador,
       Lucius the Roman, comes to Milford Haven
       To-morrow. Now if you could wear a mind
145   Dark as your fortune is, and but disguise
       That which, t' appear itself, must not yet be
       But by self-danger, you should tread a course
       Pretty and full of view; yea, happily, near
       The residence of Posthumus, so nigh, at least,
150   That though his actions were not visible, yet
       Report should render him hourly to your ear
       As truly as he moves.

Imogen.   O, for such means,
       Though peril to my modesty, not death on't,
       I would adventure.

Pisanio.   Well then, here's the point:
155   You must forget to be a woman; change
       Command into obedience, fear and niceness —
       The handmaids of all women, or more truly
       Woman it pretty self — into a waggish courage;
       Ready in gibes, quick-answered, saucy, and
160   As quarrelous as the weasel. Nay, you must
       Forget that rarest treasure of your cheek,
       Exposing it — but O, the harder heart!

---

141 *livers* people who live   145 *Dark* unrecognizable   146 *That* i.e. her sex
t' appear if it be revealed   147 *tread* i.e. pursue   148 *Pretty . . . view* desirable, with good prospects   *happily* (probably for *haply* = perhaps)
151 *render* give information about   153 *modesty* chastity   156 *Command*
i.e. her prerogative as the King's daughter   *niceness* fastidiousness   158 *it*
its   *waggish* roguish   159 *quick-answered* quick in reply   160 *quarrelous*
quarrelsome   162 *harder* too hard (different editors regard this as applying
to Posthumus, Pisanio, or Imogen herself)

Alack, no remedy — to the greedy touch
Of common-kissing Titan, and forget
Your laborsome and dainty trims, wherein   165
You made great Juno angry.

Imogen.   Nay, be brief.
I see into thy end and am almost
A man already.

Pisanio.   First, make yourself but like one.
Forethinking this, I have already fit —
'Tis in my cloak-bag — doublet, hat, hose, all   170
That answer to them. Would you, in their serving,
And with what imitation you can borrow
From youth of such a season, 'fore noble Lucius
Present yourself, desire his service, tell him
Wherein you're happy, which will make him know,   175
If that his head have ear in music; doubtless
With joy he will embrace you, for he's honorable,
And, doubling that, most holy. Your means abroad —
You have me, rich, and I will never fail
Beginning nor supplyment.

Imogen.   Thou art all the comfort   180
The gods will diet me with. Prithee away.
There's more to be considered, but we'll even
All that good time will give us. This attempt
I am soldier to, and will abide it with
A prince's courage. Away, I prithee.   185

Pisanio. Well, madam, we must take a short farewell,
Lest, being missed, I be suspected of

164 *Of . . . Titan* of the sun who kisses everything   165 *laborsome . . . trims* elaborate and tasteful attire   166 *angry* i.e. with jealousy   167 *end* purpose, plan   169 *Forethinking* planning for in advance   *fit* prepared   171 *answer to* match   *in their serving* with their assistance   173 *season* age   174 *his service* to work for him   175 *happy* gifted   *make him know* be convincing to him (?)   177 *embrace* receive   178 *means* i.e. of subsistence   182 *even* keep up with   184 *am soldier to* have courage for   *abide* face

Your carriage from the court. My noble mistress,
Here is a box; I had it from the Queen.
190 What's in't is precious. If you are sick at sea
Or stomach-qualmed at land, a dram of this
Will drive away distemper. To some shade,
And fit you to your manhood. May the gods
Direct you to the best.

Imogen.   Amen. I thank thee.   *Exeunt.*

III, v   *Enter Cymbeline, Queen, Cloten, Lucius, and Lords.*

Cymbeline. Thus far, and so farewell.
Lucius.   Thanks, royal sir.
My emperor hath wrote I must from hence,
And am right sorry that I must report ye
My master's enemy.
Cymbeline.   Our subjects, sir,
5 Will not endure his yoke, and for ourself
To show less sovereignty than they, must needs
Appear unkinglike.
Lucius.   So, sir. I desire of you
A conduct overland to Milford Haven.
Madam, all joy befall your Grace, and you.
10 *Cymbeline.* My lords, you are appointed for that office;
The due of honor in no point omit.
So farewell, noble Lucius.
Lucius.   Your hand, my lord.
Cloten. Receive it friendly, but from this time forth
I wear it as your enemy.
Lucius.   Sir, the event

188 *Your carriage* taking you away   192 *distemper* illness   193 *fit you to*
dress yourself for   III, v, 8 *conduct* escort   10 *office* duty   14 *event* outcome

Is yet to name the winner. Fare you well.   15
Cymbeline. Leave not the worthy Lucius, good my lords,
   Till he have crossed the Severn. Happiness!

                                    Exit Lucius &c.

Queen. He goes hence frowning, but it honors us
   That we have given him cause.
Cloten.   'Tis all the better;
   Your valiant Britons have their wishes in it.   20
Cymbeline. Lucius hath wrote already to the Emperor
   How it goes here. It fits us therefore ripely
   Our chariots and our horsemen be in readiness.
   The pow'rs that he already hath in Gallia
   Will soon be drawn to head, from whence he moves   25
   His war for Britain.
Queen.   'Tis not sleepy business,
   But must be looked to speedily and strongly.
Cymbeline. Our expectation that it would be thus
   Hath made us forward. But, my gentle queen,
   Where is our daughter? She hath not appeared   30
   Before the Roman, nor to us hath tendered
   The duty of the day. She looks us like
   A thing more made of malice than of duty.
   We have noted it. Call her before us, for
   We have been too slight in sufferance. *[Exit a Messenger.]*
Queen.   Royal sir,   35
   Since the exile of Posthumus, most retired
   Hath her life been; the cure whereof, my lord,
   'Tis time must do. Beseech your Majesty,

18 *it honors us* it is to our credit (i.e. we have been patriotic) 20 *have ...
it* i.e. approve our course 22 *fits* befits *ripely* fully (cf. 'the time is
ripe') 25 *drawn to head* organized, mobilized 26 *sleepy* sleep-permitting
(cf. 'asleep on the job') 29 *forward* (take) early (action) 32 *us* to us
35 *slight in sufferance* weak in tolerance (of her conduct) 36 *retired* withdrawn, unsocial

Forbear sharp speeches to her. She's a lady
40   So tender of rebukes that words are strokes,
And strokes death to her.

Enter a Messenger.

Cymbeline.   Where is she, sir? How
Can her contempt be answered?
Messenger.   Please you, sir,
Her chambers are all locked, and there's no answer
That will be given to th' loud of noise we make.
45 *Queen.* My lord, when last I went to visit her,
She prayed me to excuse her keeping close;
Whereto constrained by her infirmity,
She should that duty leave unpaid to you
Which daily she was bound to proffer. This
50   She wished me to make known, but our great court
Made me to blame in memory.
Cymbeline.   Her doors locked?
Not seen of late? Grant, heavens, that which I fear
Prove false!   *Exit.*
Queen.   Son, I say, follow the King.
Cloten. That man of hers, Pisanio, her old servant,
I have not seen these two days.
55 *Queen.*   Go, look after. *Exit [Cloten].*
Pisanio, thou that stand'st so for Posthumus —
He hath a drug of mine. I pray his absence
Proceed by swallowing that, for he believes
It is a thing most precious. But for her,
60   Where is she gone? Haply despair hath seized her,

40 *tender of* sensitive to   42 *answered* accounted for   44 *loud* loudness
(some editors emend *loud of* to *loudest*)   46 *close* to herself   47 *constrained*
compelled   *infirmity* ill-being, poor condition   50 *great court* important
session of court   51 *to blame* faulty   56 *stand'st so for* so strongly support
58 *Proceed by* result from   60 *Haply* perhaps

Or, winged with fervor of her love, she's flown
To her desired Posthumus. Gone she is
To death or to dishonor, and my end
Can make good use of either. She being down,
I have the placing of the British crown.   65

Enter Cloten.

How now, my son?
Cloten.   'Tis certain she is fled.
Go in and cheer the King. He rages; none
Dare come about him.
Queen.   [*aside*] All the better. May
This night forestall him of the coming day!   *Exit.*
Cloten. I love and hate her, for she's fair and royal,   70
And that she hath all courtly parts more exquisite
Than lady, ladies, woman. From every one
The best she hath, and she, of all compounded,
Outsells them all. I love her therefore, but
Disdaining me and throwing favors on   75
The low Posthumus slanders so her judgment
That what's else rare is choked; and in that point
I will conclude to hate her, nay, indeed,
To be revenged upon her. For, when fools
Shall —

Enter Pisanio.

            Who is here? What, are you packing, sirrah?   80
Come hither. Ah, you precious pander! Villain,
Where is thy lady? In a word, or else
Thou art straightway with the fiends.

69 *forestall* deprive   70 *for* because   71 *that* because   *parts* qualities
74 *Outsells* outvalues   75 *Disdaining* her disdaining   76 *slanders* disgraces
77 *what's else rare* her other rare qualities   80 *packing* plotting

   Pisanio.   O good my lord!
   Cloten. Where is thy lady? Or – by Jupiter,
85   I will not ask again. Close villain,
   I'll have this secret from thy heart, or rip
   Thy heart to find it. Is she with Posthumus?
   From whose so many weights of baseness cannot
   A dram of worth be drawn.
   Pisanio.   Alas, my lord,
90   How can she be with him? When was she missed?
   He is in Rome.
   Cloten.   Where is she, sir? Come nearer.
   No farther halting. Satisfy me home
   What is become of her.
   Pisanio. O my all-worthy lord!
   Cloten.   All-worthy villain!
95   Discover where thy mistress is at once,
   At the next word. No more of 'worthy lord'!
   Speak, or thy silence on the instant is
   Thy condemnation and thy death.
   Pisanio.   Then, sir,
   This paper is the history of my knowledge
   Touching her flight.   *[Presents a letter.]*
100 *Cloten.*   Let's see't. I will pursue her
   Even to Augustus' throne.
   Pisanio.   *[aside]* Or this, or perish.
   She's far enough, and what he learns by this
   May prove his travel, not her danger.
   Cloten.   Humh!
   Pisanio. [aside] I'll write to my lord she's dead. O Imogen,

---

85 *Close* secretive   89 *drawn* extracted   91 *nearer* i.e. to the point
92 *home* completely   95 *Discover* reveal   97–98 *silence … condemnation*
silence will condemn you instantly   100 *Touching* concerning   101 *Or*
either   103 *travel* difficulty, trouble

Safe mayst thou wander, safe return again!   105
Cloten. Sirrah, is this letter true?
Pisanio. Sir, as I think.
Cloten. It is Posthumus' hand; I know't. Sirrah, if thou
wouldst not be a villain, but do me true service, undergo
those employments wherein I should have cause to use   110
thee with a serious industry — that is, what villainy soe'er
I bid thee do, to perform it directly and truly — I would
think thee an honest man. Thou shouldst neither want
my means for thy relief nor my voice for thy preferment.
Pisanio. Well, my good lord.   115
Cloten. Wilt thou serve me? For since patiently and constantly thou hast stuck to the bare fortune of that beggar
Posthumus, thou canst not, in the course of gratitude,
but be a diligent follower of mine. Wilt thou serve me?
Pisanio. Sir, I will.   120
Cloten. Give me thy hand. Here's my purse. Hast any of
thy late master's garments in thy possession?
Pisanio. I have, my lord, at my lodging the same suit he
wore when he took leave of my lady and mistress.
Cloten. The first service thou dost me, fetch that suit hither. 125
Let it be thy first service. Go.
Pisanio. I shall, my lord.   *Exit.*
Cloten. Meet thee at Milford Haven! I forgot to ask him
one thing; I'll remember't anon. Even there, thou villain
Posthumus, will I kill thee. I would these garments were   130
come. She said upon a time — the bitterness of it I now
belch from my heart — that she held the very garment of
Posthumus in more respect than my noble and natural
person, together with the adornment of my qualities.

109 *undergo* undertake   111 *industry* application   114 *relief* assistance
voice support   *preferment* advancement   118 *course* ordinary action
134 *qualities* talents

135 With that suit upon my back will I ravish her; first kill
him, and in her eyes. There shall she see my valor, which
will then be a torment to her contempt. He on the
ground, my speech of insultment ended on his dead body,
and when my lust hath dined — which, as I say, to vex
140 her I will execute in the clothes that she so praised — to
the court I'll knock her back, foot her home again. She
hath despised me rejoicingly, and I'll be merry in my
revenge.

Enter Pisanio [with the clothes].

Be those the garments?
145 *Pisanio.* Ay, my noble lord.
Cloten. How long is't since she went to Milford Haven?
Pisanio. She can scarce be there yet.
Cloten. Bring this apparel to my chamber; that is the sec-
ond thing that I have commanded thee. The third is that
150 thou wilt be a voluntary mute to my design. Be but
duteous, and true preferment shall tender itself to thee.
My revenge is now at Milford. Would I had wings to
follow it! Come, and be true.   *Exit.*
Pisanio. Thou bid'st me to my loss, for true to thee
155 Were to prove false, which I will never be,
To him that is most true. To Milford go,
And find not her whom thou pursuest. Flow, flow,
You heavenly blessings, on her. This fool's speed
Be crossed with slowness; labor be his meed.   *Exit.*

137 *to her contempt* to her because of her contempt for me   138 *insultment*
triumph and scorn   141 *foot* kick   150 *be . . . mute to* be willing to keep
quiet about (as if mute)   154 *to my loss* to lose my honor   156 *him* i.e.
Posthumus, whom Pisanio thinks misled rather than untrue   159 *crossed*
thwarted   *meed* reward

Enter Imogen alone [in boy's clothes].

Imogen. I see a man's life is a tedious one.
I have tired myself, and for two nights together
Have made the ground my bed. I should be sick
But that my resolution helps me. Milford,
When from the mountain top Pisanio showed thee,   5
Thou wast within a ken. O Jove, I think
Foundations fly the wretched — such, I mean,
Where they should be relieved. Two beggars told me
I could not miss my way. Will poor folks lie,
That have afflictions on them, knowing 'tis   10
A punishment or trial? Yes. No wonder,
When rich ones scarce tell true. To lapse in fulness
Is sorer than to lie for need, and falsehood
Is worse in kings than beggars. My dear lord,
Thou art one o' th' false ones. Now I think on thee   15
My hunger 's gone, but even before, I was
At point to sink for food. But what is this?
Here is a path to't. 'Tis some savage hold.
I were best not call; I dare not call. Yet famine,
Ere clean it o'erthrow nature, makes it valiant.   20
Plenty and peace breeds cowards; hardness ever
Of hardiness is mother. Ho! Who's here?
If anything that's civil, speak; if savage,
Take or lend. Ho! No answer? Then I'll enter.
Best draw my sword, and if mine enemy   25

III, vi, 6 *ken* sight 7 *Foundations* (pun on the meanings 'security' and 'charitable organizations') 11 *trial* test (of faith or moral quality) 12 *lapse in
fulness* lie when well-to-do 13 *sorer* worse 16 *even* just 17 *At point*
about *for* for lack of 18 *hold* stronghold 19 *were best* had better
20 *clean* completely *nature* i.e. a person 21 *hardness* hardship 22 *hardiness* courage, endurance 24 *Take or lend* i.e. she expects the civil person to
speak, the savage to act, be it to take (life or money) or give (food or blows)

But fear the sword like me, he'll scarcely look on't.
Such a foe, good heavens!   *Exit [into the cave].*

Enter Belarius, Guiderius, and Arviragus.

Belarius. You, Polydore, have proved best woodman and
Are master of the feast. Cadwal and I
30   Will play the cook and servant; 'tis our match.
The sweat of industry would dry and die
But for the end it works to. Come, our stomachs
Will make what's homely savory. Weariness
Can snore upon the flint when resty sloth
35   Finds the down pillow hard. Now peace be here,
Poor house, that keep'st thyself.
Guiderius.   I am throughly weary.
Arviragus. I am weak with toil, yet strong in appetite.
Guiderius. There is cold meat i' th' cave. We'll browse on
     that
Whilst what we have killed be cooked.
Belarius.   *[looking into the cave]* Stay, come not in.
40   But that it eats our victuals, I should think
Here were a fairy.
Guiderius.   What's the matter, sir?
Belarius. By Jupiter, an angel! or, if not,
An earthly paragon! Behold divineness
No elder than a boy!

Enter Imogen.

45 *Imogen.* Good masters, harm me not.
Before I entered here, I called and thought
To have begged or bought what I have took. Good troth,

---

27 *Such . . . heavens* heavens grant me such a foe   28 *woodman* hunter
30 *match* bargain   33 *homely* plain   34 *resty* lazy   36 *keep'st* takest care of
throughly thoroughly   38 *browse* nibble   47 *Good troth* in truth

I have stol'n naught, nor would not, though I had found
Gold strewed i' th' floor. Here's money for my meat.
I would have left it on the board so soon   50
As I had made my meal, and parted
With pray'rs for the provider.

Guiderius.   Money, youth?

Arviragus. All gold and silver rather turn to dirt,
As 'tis no better reckoned but of those
Who worship dirty gods.

Imogen.   I see you're angry.   55
Know, if you kill me for my fault, I should
Have died had I not made it.

Belarius.   Whither bound?

Imogen. To Milford Haven.

Belarius. What's your name?

Imogen. Fidele, sir. I have a kinsman who   60
Is bound for Italy; he embarked at Milford;
To whom being going, almost spent with hunger,
I am fall'n in this offense.

Belarius.   Prithee, fair youth,
Think us no churls, nor measure our good minds
By this rude place we live in. Well encountered!   65
'Tis almost night; you shall have better cheer
Ere you depart, and thanks to stay and eat it.
Boys, bid him welcome.

Guiderius.   Were you a woman, youth,
I should woo hard but be your groom in honesty.
I bid for you as I do buy.

Arviragus.   I'll make 't my comfort   70

54 *of* by   62 *spent* exhausted   63 *in* into   66 *cheer* entertainment
67 *thanks to* i.e. we'll be pleased to have you   69 *but be* but to be   70 *I bid
... buy* (literal meaning not clear; the idea is that he sets a high value on
Fidele, as in making a serious bid for purchase)

He is a man. I'll love him as my brother,
And such a welcome as I'ld give to him
After long absence, such is yours. Most welcome.
Be sprightly, for you fall 'mongst friends.

Imogen.   'Mongst friends?
75 If brothers. *[aside]* Would it had been so that they
Had been my father's sons! Then had my prize
Been less, and so more equal ballasting
To thee, Posthumus.

Belarius.   He wrings at some distress.

Guiderius. Would I could free't!

Arviragus.   Or I, whate'er it be,
What pain it cost, what danger. Gods!

80 *Belarius.*   Hark, boys. *[Whispers.]*

Imogen. Great men
That had a court no bigger than this cave,
That did attend themselves and had the virtue
Which their own conscience sealed them, laying by
85 That nothing-gift of differing multitudes,
Could not outpeer these twain. Pardon me, gods,
I'ld change my sex to be companion with them,
Since Leonatus' false.

Belarius.   It shall be so.
Boys, we'll go dress our hunt. Fair youth, come in.
90 Discourse is heavy, fasting. When we have supped,
We'll mannerly demand thee of thy story,
So far as thou wilt speak it.

Guiderius.   Pray draw near.

74 *sprightly* in good spirits   76 *prize* (pun on the meanings 'value' and
'captured ship')   77 *less* i.e. she would not have been heir to the throne
ballasting weight, position   78 *wrings* writhes   83 *attend* serve   84 *laying
by* disregarding   85 *nothing-gift* worthless gift (admission? attendance?)
differing inconsistent   86 *outpeer* excel   89 *dress our hunt* prepare our game
90 *Discourse . . . fasting* conversation is burdensome when we have not eaten

Arviragus. The night to th' owl and morn to th' lark less
    welcome.
Imogen. Thanks, sir.
Arviragus. I pray draw near.   *Exeunt.* 95

Enter two Roman Senators, and Tribunes.   III, vii

1. Senator. This is the tenor of the Emperor's writ:
    That since the common men are now in action
    'Gainst the Pannonians and Dalmatians,
    And that the legions now in Gallia are
    Full weak to undertake our wars against   5
    The fall'n-off Britons, that we do incite
    The gentry to this business. He creates
    Lucius proconsul, and to you the tribunes,
    For this immediate levy, he commands
    His absolute commission. Long live Caesar!   10
Tribune. Is Lucius general of the forces?
2. Senator.   Ay.
Tribune. Remaining now in Gallia?
1. Senator.   With those legions
    Which I have spoke of, whereunto your levy
    Must be supplyant. The words of your commission
    Will tie you to the numbers and the time   15
    Of their dispatch.
Tribune.   We will discharge our duty.   *Exeunt.*

III, vii, 1 *writ* dispatch 5 *Full* quite 6 *fall'n-off* revolted *incite* sum-
mon 9 *commands* entrusts 10 *commission* authority 14 *supplyant* sup-
plementary 15 *tie you to* specify to you

115

Enter Cloten alone.

Cloten. I am near to th' place where they should meet, if
Pisanio have mapped it truly. How fit his garments serve
me! Why should his mistress, who was made by him
that made the tailor, not be fit too? The rather, saving
5   reverence of the word, for 'tis said a woman's fitness
comes by fits. Therein I must play the workman. I dare
speak it to myself, for it is not vainglory for a man and
his glass to confer in his own chamber – I mean, the lines
of my body are as well drawn as his; no less young, more
10 strong, not beneath him in fortunes, beyond him in the
advantage of the time, above him in birth, alike conversant in general services, and more remarkable in single
oppositions. Yet this imperceiverant thing loves him in
my despite. What mortality is! Posthumus, thy head,
15 which now is growing upon thy shoulders, shall within
this hour be off, thy mistress enforced, thy garments cut
to pieces before thy face; and all this done, spurn her
home to her father, who may happily be a little angry
for my so rough usage; but my mother, having power
20 of his testiness, shall turn all into my commendations. My
horse is tied up safe. Out, sword, and to a sore purpose!
Fortune put them into my hand. This is the very description of their meeting place, and the fellow dares not
deceive me.   *Exit.*

IV, i, 2 *fit* fittingly   4 *fit* i.e. for me (with pun on the meaning 'inclined
to')   4–5 *saving reverence* with all due respect to you (apology to audience
for puns on *fit*)   5 *for* since   *fitness* inclination (i.e. sexual)   6 *fits* (cf.
'fits and starts')   8 *glass* mirror   11 *of the time* in the present (social)
world   11–12 *alike conversant* equally experienced   12 *services* i.e. military
13 *oppositions* combats   *imperceiverant* unperceiving   14 *What mortality is*
what a thing life is   16 *enforced* raped   17 *thy face* (some editors emend
thy to *her*)   *spurn* kick   18 *happily* (as elsewhere, for *haply,* perchance)
19–20 *power of* control over   20 *commendations* credit   21 *sore* causing
pain   22 *This is* this place fits

116

Enter Belarius, Guiderius, Arviragus, and Imogen from IV, ii
  the cave.

Belarius. [to Imogen] You are not well. Remain here in the
    cave;
  We'll come to you after hunting.
Arviragus. [to Imogen]   Brother, stay here.
  Are we not brothers?
Imogen.   So man and man should be,
  But clay and clay differs in dignity,
  Whose dust is both alike. I am very sick.   5
Guiderius. Go you to hunting; I'll abide with him.
Imogen. So sick I am not, yet I am not well,
  But not so citizen a wanton as
  To seem to die ere sick. So please you, leave me;
  Stick to your journal course; the breach of custom   10
  Is breach of all. I am ill, but your being by me
  Cannot amend me; society is no comfort
  To one not sociable. I am not very sick,
  Since I can reason of it. Pray you trust me here —
  I'll rob none but myself — and let me die,   15
  Stealing so poorly.
Guiderius.   I love thee — I have spoke it —
  How much the quantity, the weight as much
  As I do love my father.
Belarius.   What? How, how?
Arviragus. If it be sin to say so, sir, I yoke me
  In my good brother's fault. I know not why   20

IV, ii, 4 *clay and clay* different persons 5 *dust* remains after death 8 *citizen* city-bred (cf. 'citified,' 'sissy') *wanton* spoiled child 10 *journal* daily, regular *breach* disruption 12 *amend* make better 16 *poorly* i.e. from myself only 17 *How . . . as much* as much, as deeply 19–20 *yoke . . . fault* confess to having committed the same fault as my brother

I love this youth, and I have heard you say
Love's reason's without reason. The bier at door,
And a demand who is't shall die, I'ld say
'My father, not this youth.'

Belarius.   [*aside*] O noble strain!

25   O worthiness of nature, breed of greatness!
Cowards father cowards and base things sire base;
Nature hath meal and bran, contempt and grace.
I'm not their father; yet who this should be
Doth miracle itself, loved before me. —
'Tis the ninth hour o' th' morn.

30 *Arviragus.*   Brother, farewell.

Imogen. I wish ye sport.

Arviragus.   You health. [*to Belarius*] So please
you, sir.

Imogen. [*aside*] These are kind creatures. Gods, what lies I
have heard!
Our courtiers say all's savage but at court.
Experience, O, thou disprov'st report!

35   Th' imperious seas breeds monsters; for the dish
Poor tributary rivers as sweet fish.
I am sick still, heartsick. Pisanio,
I'll now taste of thy drug.   [*Swallows some.*]

Guiderius.   I could not stir him.
He said he was gentle, but unfortunate;

40   Dishonestly afflicted, but yet honest.

---

24 *strain* lineage, heredity   26, 27 (in the folio text, these lines are introduced by quotation marks to identify them as maxims or well-known say-
ings)   28–29 *who ... me* that this person, whoever he may be, should be
loved ahead of me is miraculous   31 *So please you* at your command
35 *imperious* imperial   36 *rivers ... fish* rivers (breed) just as sweet fish (as
the sea does)   38 *stir* move (to tell about himself)   39 *gentle* of noble birth

Arviragus. Thus did he answer me, yet said hereafter
  I might know more.
Belarius.   To th' field, to th' field.
  [*To Imogen*] We'll leave you for this time; go in and rest.
Arviragus. We'll not be long away.
Belarius.   Pray be not sick,
  For you must be our housewife.
Imogen.   Well or ill,   45
  I am bound to you.   *Exit [into the cave].*
Belarius.   And shalt be ever.
  This youth, howe'er distressed, appears he hath had
  Good ancestors.
Arviragus.   How angel-like he sings!
Guiderius. But his neat cookery! He cut our roots in
    characters,
  And sauced our broths as Juno had been sick   50
  And he her dieter.
Arviragus.   Nobly he yokes
  A smiling with a sigh, as if the sigh
  Was that it was for not being such a smile;
  The smile mocking the sigh that it would fly
  From so divine a temple to commix   55
  With winds that sailors rail at.
Guiderius.   I do note
  That grief and patience, rooted in them both,
  Mingle their spurs together.
Arviragus.   Grow patience,
  And let the stinking elder, grief, untwine

---

46 *bound* obligated   *shalt be* i.e. bound (by emotional ties)   49 *neat* **fine,**
elegant   *characters* letters (of the alphabet); designs   50 *as* as if   51 *dieter*
dietitian   53 *that* what   57 *them* i.e. the smile and sigh (some **editors**
emend to *him*)   58 *spurs* roots   59 *elder* elder tree

60   His perishing root with the increasing vine.
Belarius. It is great morning. Come away. Who's there?

Enter Cloten.

Cloten. I cannot find those runagates. That villain
       Hath mocked me. I am faint.
Belarius.   'Those runagates'?
       Means he not us? I partly know him. 'Tis
65   Cloten, the son o' th' Queen. I fear some ambush.
       I saw him not these many years, and yet
       I know 'tis he. We are held as outlaws. Hence!
Guiderius. He is but one. You and my brother search
       What companies are near. Pray you, away.
       Let me alone with him. *[Exeunt Belarius and Arviragus.]*
70 *Cloten.*   Soft, what are you
       That fly me thus? Some villain mountaineers?
       I have heard of such. What slave art thou?
Guiderius.   A thing
       More slavish did I ne'er than answering
       A 'slave' without a knock.
Cloten.   Thou art a robber,
75   A lawbreaker, a villain. Yield thee, thief.
Guiderius. To who? To thee? What art thou? Have not I
       An arm as big as thine? A heart as big?
       Thy words, I grant, are bigger, for I wear not
       My dagger in my mouth. Say what thou art,
       Why I should yield to thee.
80 *Cloten.*   Thou villain base,

---

60 *perishing* noxious *with ... vine* from the increasing vine (?) as the vine
increases (?) 61 *great morning* broad daylight 62 *runagates* runaways
63 *mocked* fooled 67 *held* regarded 69 *companies* followers 70 *Soft*
stop (exclamation; cf. 'take it easy') 74 *'slave'* (Guiderius may be quot-
ing Cloten's word or simply calling Cloten a slave)

Know'st me not by my clothes?

Guiderius.   No, nor thy tailor, rascal,
Who is thy grandfather. He made those clothes,
Which, as it seems, make thee.

Cloten.   Thou precious varlet,
My tailor made them not.

Guiderius.   Hence then, and thank
The man that gave them thee. Thou art some fool;   85
I am loath to beat thee.

Cloten.   Thou injurious thief,
Hear but my name and tremble.

Guiderius.   What's thy name?

Cloten. Cloten, thou villain.

Guiderius. Cloten, thou double villain, be thy name,
I cannot tremble at it. Were it Toad, or Adder, Spider,   90
'Twould move me sooner.

Cloten.   To thy further fear,
Nay, to thy mere confusion, thou shalt know
I am son to th' Queen.

Guiderius.   I am sorry for't; not seeming
So worthy as thy birth.

Cloten.   Art not afeard?

Guiderius. Those that I reverence, those I fear – the wise;   95
At fools I laugh, not fear them.

Cloten.   Die the death!
When I have slain thee with my proper hand,
I'll follow those that even now fled hence
And on the gates of Lud's town set your heads.
Yield, rustic mountaineer.   *Fight and exeunt.*   100

---

81 *clothes* i.e. court clothes   83 *varlet* knave   86 *injurious* insulting
92 *mere confusion* utter destruction   93 *not seeming* since you do not seem
96 *Die the death* (as if he were imposing a legal sentence)   97 *proper* own

Enter Belarius and Arviragus.

Belarius. No company's abroad?

Arviragus. None in the world. You did mistake him sure.

Belarius. I cannot tell. Long is it since I saw him,
But time hath nothing blurred those lines of favor
105 Which then he wore. The snatches in his voice,
And burst of speaking, were as his. I am absolute
'Twas very Cloten.

Arviragus.   In this place we left them.
I wish my brother make good time with him,
You say he is so fell.

Belarius.   Being scarce made up,
110 I mean to man, he had not apprehension
Of roaring terrors; for defect of judgment
Is oft the cause of fear.

Enter Guiderius [with Cloten's head].

                          But see, thy brother.

Guiderius. This Cloten was a fool, an empty purse;
There was no money in't. Not Hercules
115 Could have knocked out his brains, for he had none.
Yet I not doing this, the fool had borne
My head as I do his.

---

101 *abroad* around, in the neighborhood   104 *lines of favor* facial lines
105 *snatches* catches, hesitations   106 *absolute* positive   107 *very Cloten*
Cloten himself   108 *make good time* may succeed (cf. 'have a good day')
109 *fell* savage   *made up* grown up (in sense of years or mental ability)
110 *apprehension* understanding   111–12 *defect . . . fear* (1) some editors
think that there is a scribal or typographic error, such as *cause* for *cease;*
(2) other editors, that Shakespeare wrote these words but was careless about
meaning; (3) others, that Shakespeare wrote the words and intended this
meaning: Cloten was fearless because he had no wits at all instead of some
wits defectively used ('defect of judgment')

Belarius.   What hast thou done?
Guiderius. I am perfect what: cut off one Cloten's head,
    Son to the Queen, after his own report;
    Who called me traitor, mountaineer, and swore   120
    With his own single hand he'ld take us in,
    Displace our heads where – thank the gods – they grow,
    And set them on Lud's town.
Belarius.   We are all undone.
Guiderius. Why, worthy father, what have we to lose
    But that he swore to take, our lives? The law   125
    Protects not us. Then why should we be tender
    To let an arrogant piece of flesh threat us,
    Play judge and executioner all himself,
    For we do fear the law? What company
    Discover you abroad?
Belarius.   No single soul   130
    Can we set eye on, but in all safe reason
    He must have some attendants. Though his honor
    Was nothing but mutation – ay, and that
    From one bad thing to worse – not frenzy, not
    Absolute madness could so far have raved   135
    To bring him here alone. Although perhaps
    It may be heard at court that such as we
    Cave here, hunt here, are outlaws, and in time
    May make some stronger head; the which he hearing –
    As it is like him – might break out, and swear   140
    He'ld fetch us in; yet is 't not probable
    To come alone, either he so undertaking,

---

118 *perfect* aware   121 *take us in* subdue us   125 *that* what   126–27 *tender To* so tolerant as to   129 *For* because   132 *honor* (implies steadfastness; ironically joined with *mutation,* changeableness. Some editors emend to *humor.*)   139 *make . . . head* become a stronger force   141 *fetch us in* capture us   142 *To come* for him to come

Or they so suffering. Then on good ground we fear,
If we do fear this body hath a tail
More perilous than the head.
145 *Arviragus.*   Let ordinance
Come as the gods foresay it. Howsoe'er,
My brother hath done well.
Belarius.   I had no mind
To hunt this day. The boy Fidele's sickness
Did make my way long forth.
Guiderius.   With his own sword,
150 Which he did wave against my throat, I have ta'en
His head from him. I'll throw't into the creek
Behind our rock, and let it to the sea
And tell the fishes he's the Queen's son, Cloten.
That's all I reck.   *Exit.*
Belarius.   I fear 'twill be revenged.
Would, Polydore, thou hadst not done't, though
155   valor
Becomes thee well enough.
Arviragus.   Would I had done't,
So the revenge alone pursued me. Polydore,
I love thee brotherly, but envy much
Thou hast robbed me of this deed. I would revenges
160 That possible strength might meet would seek us through
And put us to our answer.
Belarius.   Well, 'tis done.
We'll hunt no more to-day, nor seek for danger
Where there's no profit. I prithee, to our rock;
You and Fidele play the cooks. I'll stay

143 *suffering* permitting (it)   144 *tail* i.e. what comes after: followers hostile to us   145 *ordinance* whatever is ordained   149 *Did . . . forth* made my walk forth (from the cave) seem long   154 *reck* care   157 *So* so that   *pursued* would have pursued   160 *possible* our available   *meet* i.e. in combat   *seek us through* come upon us   161 *put* force

124

Till hasty Polydore return, and bring him   165
To dinner presently.
Arviragus.   Poor sick Fidele,
I'll willingly to him. To gain his color
I'ld let a parish of such Clotens blood
And praise myself for charity.   *Exit.*
Belarius.   O thou goddess,
Thou divine Nature, thou thyself thou blazon'st   170
In these two princely boys! They are as gentle
As zephyrs blowing below the violet,
Not wagging his sweet head; and yet as rough,
Their royal blood enchafed, as the rud'st wind
That by the top doth take the mountain pine   175
And make him stoop to th' vale. 'Tis wonder
That an invisible instinct should frame them
To royalty unlearned, honor untaught,
Civility not seen from other, valor
That wildly grows in them but yields a crop   180
As if it had been sowed. Yet still it's strange
What Cloten's being here to us portends,
Or what his death will bring us.

Enter Guiderius.

Guiderius.   Where's my brother?
I have sent Cloten's clotpoll down the stream
In embassy to his mother; his body's hostage   185
For his return.   *Solemn music.*
Belarius.   My ingenious instrument!

165 *hasty* quick to act   167 *gain his color* restore the color (to) his (cheeks)
168 *let ... blood* let blood for a parish of such Clotens (a medical term
as a metaphor for 'kill')   170 *blazon'st* depictest   174 *enchafed* heated
177 *frame* direct   178 *royalty* kingly conduct   179 *Civility* civilized
conduct   180 *wildly* spontaneously   184 *clotpoll* blockhead   186 *ingenious* skillfully constructed

Hark, Polydore, it sounds. But what occasion
Hath Cadwal now to give it motion? Hark!
Guiderius. Is he at home?
Belarius.   He went hence even now.
Guiderius. What does he mean? Since death of my dear'st
190   mother
It did not speak before. All solemn things
Should answer solemn accidents. The matter?
Triumphs for nothing and lamenting toys
Is jollity for apes and grief for boys.
Is Cadwal mad?

Enter Arviragus, with Imogen dead, bearing her in his arms.

195 *Belarius.*   Look, here he comes,
And brings the dire occasion in his arms
Of what we blame him for.
Arviragus.   The bird is dead
That we have made so much on. I had rather
Have skipped from sixteen years of age to sixty,
200   To have turned my leaping time into a crutch,
Than have seen this.
Guiderius.   O sweetest, fairest lily!
My brother wears thee not the one half so well
As when thou grew'st thyself.
Belarius.   O melancholy,
Who ever yet could sound thy bottom, find
205   The ooze, to show what coast thy sluggish crare
Might eas'liest harbor in? Thou blessèd thing,
Jove knows what man thou mightst have made; but I,

188 *give it motion* play it   189 *even* just   192 *answer* correspond to   *accidents* events   193 *lamenting toys* lamenting for trifles   198 *on* of   204 *sound
thy bottom* measure thy depths   205 *crare* small boat   206 *thing* i.e. Fidele
207 *but I* but I know that

Thou diedst, a most rare boy, of melancholy.
How found you him?

Arviragus.   Stark, as you see,
Thus smiling, as some fly had tickled slumber,   210
Not as death's dart being laughed at; his right cheek
Reposing on a cushion.

Guiderius.   Where?

Arviragus.   O' th' floor;
His arms thus leagued. I thought he slept, and put
My clouted brogues from off my feet, whose rudeness
Answered my steps too loud.

Guiderius.   Why, he but sleeps.   215
If he be gone, he'll make his grave a bed;
With female fairies will his tomb be haunted,
And worms will not come to thee.

Arviragus.   With fairest flowers,
Whilst summer lasts and I live here, Fidele,
I'll sweeten thy sad grave. Thou shalt not lack   220
The flower that's like thy face, pale primrose; nor
The azured harebell, like thy veins; no, nor
The leaf of eglantine, whom not to slander,
Outsweet'ned not thy breath. The ruddock would
With charitable bill — O bill, sore shaming   225
Those rich-left heirs that let their fathers lie
Without a monument! — bring thee all this,
Yea, and furred moss besides. When flowers are none
To winter-ground thy corse —

Guiderius.   Prithee have done,

209 *Stark* stiff (in rigor mortis) 210 *as* as if 211 *as ... at* as if the
sting of death were being laughed at 213 *leagued* crossed 214 *clouted
brogues* nail-studded boots *rudeness* coarseness (of the boots) 222 *azured*
sky-blue 224 *ruddock* robin 229 *To winter-ground* to protect in winter (?)
(or it may be a prepositional phrase belonging to uncompleted predicate
of interrupted sentence)

230   And do not play in wench-like words with that
       Which is so serious. Let us bury him,
       And not protract with admiration what
       Is now due debt. To th' grave.
       Arviragus.   Say, where shall's lay him?
       Guiderius. By good Euriphile, our mother.
       Arviragus.   Be't so.
235   And let us, Polydore, though now our voices
       Have got the mannish crack, sing him to th' ground,
       As once to our mother; use like note and words,
       Save that Euriphile must be Fidele.
       Guiderius. Cadwal,
240   I cannot sing. I'll weep, and word it with thee,
       For notes of sorrow out of tune are worse
       Than priests and fanes that lie.
       Arviragus.   We'll speak it then.
       Belarius. Great griefs, I see, med'cine the less, for Cloten
       Is quite forgot. He was a queen's son, boys,
245   And though he came our enemy, remember
       He was paid for that. Though mean and mighty, rotting
       Together, have one dust, yet reverence,
       That angel of the world, doth make distinction
       Of place 'tween high and low. Our foe was princely,
250   And though you took his life as being our foe,
       Yet bury him as a prince.
       Guiderius.   Pray you fetch him hither.
       Thersites' body is as good as Ajax'
       When neither are alive.
       Arviragus.   If you'll go fetch him,

230 *wench-like* womanish   233 *shall's* shall us (we)   236 *crack* break, tone
240 *word* speak, recite   242 *fanes* temples   246 *paid* punished   248 *angel*
. . . *world* messenger sent from heaven to earth   250 *as being* because he was
252 *Thersites* vindictive and foul-mouthed Greek   *Ajax* Greek hero

We'll say our song the whilst. Brother, begin.

[*Exit Belarius.*]

Guiderius. Nay, Cadwal, we must lay his head to th' east;   255
My father hath a reason for't.

Arviragus.   'Tis true.

Guiderius. Come on then and remove him.

Arviragus.   So. Begin.

                    Song.

Guiderius.   Fear no more the heat o' th' sun
                        Nor the furious winter's rages;
                    Thou thy worldly task hast done,   260
                        Home art gone and ta'en thy wages.
                    Golden lads and girls all must,
                    As chimney-sweepers, come to dust.

Arviragus.   Fear no more the frown o' th' great;
                    Thou art past the tyrant's stroke.   265
                    Care no more to clothe and eat;
                        To thee the reed is as the oak.
                    The scepter, learning, physic, must
                    All follow this and come to dust.

Guiderius.   Fear no more the lightning flash,   270
Arviragus.   Nor th' all-dreaded thunder-stone;
Guiderius.   Fear no slander, censure rash;
Arviragus.   Thou hast finished joy and moan.
Both.   All lovers young, all lovers must
                    Consign to thee and come to dust.   275

255 *to th' east* (the opposite of Christian practice; a way of suggesting the non-Christian world of the play) 262 *Golden* i.e. fine 263 *As* like 268 *scepter, learning, physic* kings, scholars, doctors 271 *thunder-stone* thunderbolt 275 *Consign* perhaps, co-sign (i.e. the same contract: meet the same fate)

Guiderius.	No exorciser harm thee,
Arviragus.	Nor no witchcraft charm thee.
Guiderius.	Ghost unlaid forbear thee;
Arviragus.	Nothing ill come near thee.
280 *Both.*	Quiet consummation have,
	And renownèd be thy grave.

Enter Belarius with the body of Cloten.

Guiderius. We have done our obsequies. Come, lay him
    down.
Belarius. Here's a few flowers, but 'bout midnight, more.
    The herbs that have on them cold dew o' th' night
285   Are strewings fitt'st for graves. Upon their faces.
    You were as flow'rs, now withered; even so
    These herblets shall which we upon you strew.
    Come on, away; apart upon our knees.
    The ground that gave them first has them again.
290   Their pleasures here are past, so is their pain.
                  Exeunt [Belarius, Guiderius, and Arviragus].

Imogen awakes.

[*Imogen.*] Yes, sir, to Milford Haven. Which is the way?
    I thank you. By yond bush? Pray, how far thither?
    'Ods pittikins, can it be six mile yet?
    I have gone all night. Faith, I'll lie down and sleep.
                      [Sees the body of Cloten.]
295   But, soft, no bedfellow! O gods and goddesses!
    These flow'rs are like the pleasures of the world;
    This bloody man, the care on't. I hope I dream,

276 *exorciser* conjurer   278 *unlaid* not driven out (by formal procedures)
forbear leave alone   280 *consummation* fulfilment (i.e. death)   285 *Upon their
faces* flowers on front of bodies (?) flowers lying face down (?)   286 *now*
now you are   287 *shall* shall be (withered)   293 *'Ods pittikins* God's little
pity (diminutive of '[I pray for] God's pity'; cf. ll. 304–5)   294 *gone* walked

For so I thought I was a cave-keeper
And cook to honest creatures. But 'tis not so;
'Twas but a bolt of nothing, shot at nothing,   300
Which the brain makes of fumes. Our very eyes
Are sometimes like our judgments, blind. Good faith,
I tremble still with fear, but if there be
Yet left in heaven as small a drop of pity
As a wren's eye, feared gods, a part of it!   305
The dream's here still. Even when I wake it is
Without me, as within me; not imagined, felt.
A headless man? The garments of Posthumus?
I know the shape of's leg; this is his hand,
His foot Mercurial, his Martial thigh,   310
The brawns of Hercules; but his Jovial face —
Murder in heaven? How? 'Tis gone. Pisanio,
All curses madded Hecuba gave the Greeks,
And mine to boot, be darted on thee! Thou,
Conspired with that irregulous devil Cloten,   315
Hath here cut off my lord. To write and read
Be henceforth treacherous! Damned Pisanio
Hath with his forgèd letters — damned Pisanio —
From this most bravest vessel of the world
Struck the maintop. O Posthumus, alas,   320
Where is thy head? Where's that? Ay me, where's that?
Pisanio might have killed thee at the heart
And left this head on. How should this be? Pisanio?

298 *so* i.e. in a dream (such as this may be) *cave-keeper* cave dweller
300 *bolt* arrow 301 *fumes* vapors believed to rise from the body to the
brain and cause dreams 305 *a part* i.e. grant me a part 310 *Mercurial*
quick, like Mercury's *Martial* powerful, like Mars's 311 *brawns* muscles
Jovial like that of Jove, king of the gods 313 *madded* maddened *Hecuba*
wife of Priam, king of Troy, destroyed by the Greeks 315 *Conspired*
conspiring *irregulous* lawless

'Tis he and Cloten. Malice and lucre in them
325　Have laid this woe here. O, 'tis pregnant, pregnant!
The drug he gave me, which he said was precious
And cordial to me, have I not found it
Murd'rous to th' senses? That confirms it home.
This is Pisanio's deed, and Cloten. O,
330　Give color to my pale cheek with thy blood,
That we the horrider may seem to those
Which chance to find us. O my lord, my lord!
　　　　　　　　　　　　　　　　[Falls on the body.]

　　　Enter Lucius, Captains, and a Soothsayer.

Captain. To them the legions garrisoned in Gallia
After your will have crossed the sea, attending
335　You here at Milford Haven with your ships.
They are here in readiness.
Lucius.　　　　　　　　　But what from Rome?
Captain. The Senate hath stirred up the confiners
And gentlemen of Italy, most willing spirits
That promise noble service, and they come
340　Under the conduct of bold Iachimo,
Siena's brother.
Lucius.　　　　　When expect you them?
Captain. With the next benefit o' th' wind.
Lucius.　　　　　　　　　　　　This forwardness
Makes our hopes fair. Command our present numbers
Be mustered; bid the captains look to't. Now, sir,

---

324 *lucre* greed　325 *pregnant* clear　327 *cordial* of medicinal value
328 *home* entirely (cf. 'drives the point home')　329 *Cloten* (idiomatic for
Cloten's)　332 *Which* who　333 *To* besides　*them* i.e. forces mentioned by
officers before coming on stage　334 *After* according to　*attending* waiting
for　337 *confiners* inhabitants　341 *Siena's* lord of Siena's　342 *forwardness*
moving ahead (on schedule)　343 *fair* strong

What have you dreamed of late of this war's purpose? 345
Soothsayer. Last night the very gods showed me a vision —
  I fast and prayed for their intelligence — thus:
  I saw Jove's bird, the Roman eagle, winged
  From the spongy south to this part of the west,
  There vanished in the sunbeams; which portends, 350
  Unless my sins abuse my divination,
  Success to th' Roman host.
Lucius.   Dream often so,
  And never false. Soft, ho, what trunk is here?
  Without his top? The ruin speaks that sometime
  It was a worthy building. How, a page? 355
  Or dead or sleeping on him? But dead rather,
  For nature doth abhor to make his bed
  With the defunct or sleep upon the dead.
  Let's see the boy's face.
Captain.   He's alive, my lord.
Lucius. He'll, then, instruct us of this body. Young one, 360
  Inform us of thy fortunes, for it seems
  They crave to be demanded. Who is this
  Thou mak'st thy bloody pillow? Or who was he
  That, otherwise than noble nature did,
  Hath altered that good picture? What's thy interest 365
  In this sad wrack? How came't? Who is't? What art
    thou?
Imogen. I am nothing, or if not,
  Nothing to be were better. This was my master,

---

345 *of late* lately *this war's purpose* our achieving our purpose in this war
347 *fast* fasted *their intelligence* information from them 349 *spongy* damp
351 *abuse* mislead 353 *false* (dream) falsely 356 *Or* either 357 *nature
doth abhor* man naturally abhors 358 *defunct* dead 360 *instruct us of* inform
us about 362 *crave ... demanded* beg to be asked about (i.e. are such as to
arouse curiosity or sympathy) 364 *otherwise ... did* from the form given
it by noble nature 366 *wrack* ruin

A very valiant Briton and a good,
370 That here by mountaineers lies slain. Alas,
There is no more such masters. I may wander
From east to occident, cry out for service,
Try many, all good, serve truly, never
Find such another master.

Lucius.   'Lack, good youth,
375 Thou mov'st no less with thy complaining than
Thy master in bleeding. Say his name, good friend.

Imogen. Richard du Champ. *[aside]* If I do lie and do
No harm by it, though the gods hear, I hope
They'll pardon it. Say you, sir?

Lucius.   Thy name?

Imogen.   Fidele, sir.

380 *Lucius.* Thou dost approve thyself the very same;
Thy name well fits thy faith, thy faith thy name.
Wilt take thy chance with me? I will not say
Thou shalt be so well mastered, but be sure
No less beloved. The Roman emperor's letters
385 Sent by a consul to me should not sooner
Than thine own worth prefer thee. Go with me.

Imogen. I'll follow, sir. But first, an't please the gods,
I'll hide my master from the flies, as deep
As these poor pickaxes can dig; and when
390 With wild wood-leaves and weeds I ha' strewed his grave
And on it said a century of prayers,
Such as I can, twice o'er, I'll weep and sigh,
And leaving so his service, follow you,
So please you entertain me.

Lucius.   Ay, good youth,

375 *mov'st no less* art no less moving 380 *approve* prove 386 *prefer* recommend 389 *pickaxes* i.e. fingers 391 *century* hundred 392 *can* know
394 *So* if it   *entertain* employ

134

And rather father thee than master thee.   395
My friends,
The boy hath taught us manly duties. Let us
Find out the prettiest daisied plot we can
And make him with our pikes and partisans
A grave. Come, arm him. Boy, he's preferred   400
By thee to us, and he shall be interred
As soldiers can. Be cheerful; wipe thine eyes.
Some falls are means the happier to arise.   *Exeunt.*

Enter Cymbeline, Lords, and Pisanio.   IV, iii

Cymbeline. Again, and bring me word how 'tis with her.
                              [Exit an Attendant.]
A fever with the absence of her son,
A madness, of which her life's in danger. Heavens,
How deeply you at once do touch me! Imogen,
The great part of my comfort, gone; my queen   5
Upon a desperate bed, and in a time
When fearful wars point at me; her son gone,
So needful for this present. It strikes me past
The hope of comfort. But for thee, fellow,
Who needs must know of her departure and   10
Dost seem so ignorant, we'll enforce it from thee
By a sharp torture.
Pisanio.   Sir, my life is yours,
I humbly set it at your will; but for my mistress,

---

399 *partisans* long-handled weapons   400 *arm him* carry him in your arms
preferred recommended   IV, iii, 4 *touch* wound   6 *desperate* i.e. she is criti-
cally ill   8 *needful* needed   *It . . . past* the blow to me is beyond   11 *enforce . . . thee* force you to talk, get it out of you

I nothing know where she remains, why gone,
15   Nor when she purposes return. Beseech your Highness,
Hold me your loyal servant.

Lord.   Good my liege,
The day that she was missing he was here.
I dare be bound he's true and shall perform
All parts of his subjection loyally. For Cloten,
20   There wants no diligence in seeking him,
And will no doubt be found.

Cymbeline.   The time is troublesome.
[To Pisanio] We'll slip you for a season, but our jealousy
Does yet depend.

Lord.   So please your Majesty,
The Roman legions, all from Gallia drawn,
25   Are landed on your coast, with a supply
Of Roman gentlemen by the senate sent.

Cymbeline. Now for the counsel of my son and queen!
I am amazed with matter.

Lord.   Good my liege,
Your preparation can affront no less
Than what you hear of. Come more, for more you're
30   ready.
The want is but to put those pow'rs in motion
That long to move.

Cymbeline.   I thank you. Let's withdraw,
And meet the time as it seeks us. We fear not
What can from Italy annoy us, but

---

16 *Hold* consider 19 *subjection* duties as a subject 21 *will* he will *trouble-some* full of troubles, seriously disturbed 22 *slip* turn loose *jealousy* suspicion 23 *depend* hang (over you) 27 *Now for* if only I now had 28 *amazed with matter* confused by (all the) business 29 *preparation* armed force *affront* confront 29–30 *no less Than* an army as large as 30 *Come more* if more come 31 *The . . . but* all that's needed is 34 *annoy* injure

We grieve at chances here. Away.   35

                                    Exeunt [all but Pisanio].

Pisanio. I heard no letter from my master since
  I wrote him Imogen was slain. 'Tis strange.
  Nor hear I from my mistress, who did promise
  To yield me often tidings. Neither know I
  What is betid to Cloten, but remain   40
  Perplexed in all. The heavens still must work.
  Wherein I am false I am honest; not true, to be true.
  These present wars shall find I love my country,
  Even to the note o' th' King, or I'll fall in them.
  All other doubts, by time let them be cleared;   45
  Fortune brings in some boats that are not steered. *Exit.*

      Enter Belarius, Guiderius, and Arviragus.   IV, iv

Guiderius. The noise is round about us.
Belarius.   Let us from it.
Arviragus. What pleasure, sir, find we in life, to lock it
  From action and adventure?
Guiderius.   Nay, what hope
  Have we in hiding us? This way the Romans
  Must or for Britons slay us or receive us   5
  For barbarous and unnatural revolts
  During their use, and slay us after.
Belarius.   Sons,
  We'll higher to the mountains, there secure us.

36 *no letter* not a whit 40 *betid* happened 44 *note* o' recognition by
IV, iv, 2 *to lock it* when it is closed off 4 *This way* i.e. if we hide 5 *Must
or* must either 5–7 *receive . . . use* i.e. accept us and use us for a time against
the British, service which for us would be barbarous and unnatural 8 *secure
us* make ourselves safe

To the King's party there's no going. Newness
10 Of Cloten's death — we being not known, not mustered
Among the bands — may drive us to a render
Where we have lived, and so extort from's that
Which we have done, whose answer would be death
Drawn on with torture.

Guiderius.   This is, sir, a doubt
15 In such a time nothing becoming you
Nor satisfying us.

Arviragus.   It is not likely
That when they hear the Roman horses neigh,
Behold their quartered fires, have both their eyes
And ears so cloyed importantly as now,
20 That they will waste their time upon our note,
To know from whence we are.

Belarius.   O, I am known
Of many in the army. Many years,
Though Cloten then but young, you see, not wore him
From my remembrance. And besides, the King
25 Hath not deserved my service nor your loves,
Who find in my exile the want of breeding,
The certainty of this hard life; aye hopeless
To have the courtesy your cradle promised,
But to be still hot summer's tanlings and
The shrinking slaves of winter.

30 *Guiderius.*   Than be so

---

9 *Newness* recency 10 *mustered* enrolled 11 *render* account 13 *whose answer* to which the reply (i.e. the penalty) 14 *Drawn on with* led up to by
18 *quartered* camp 19 *cloyed importantly* filled with important business
20 *upon our note* in noticing us 23 *then* was then *not wore* did not wear (i.e. erase) 25–26 *your . . . breeding* the love of you two who because of my exile meet with lack of cultivation 27 *certainty* inescapability 27–28 *hopeless . . . courtesy* without hope of having the courtly style 28 *cradle* birth
29 *tanlings* tanned persons, i.e. living in the open, unsheltered

Better to cease to be. Pray, sir, to th' army.
I and my brother are not known; yourself
So out of thought, and thereto so o'ergrown,
Cannot be questioned.

Arviragus.   By this sun that shines,
    I'll thither. What thing is't that I never   35
    Did see man die, scarce ever looked on blood
    But that of coward hares, hot goats, and venison!
    Never bestrid a horse, save one that had
    A rider like myself, who ne'er wore rowel
    Nor iron on his heel! I am ashamed   40
    To look upon the holy sun, to have
    The benefit of his blest beams, remaining
    So long a poor unknown.

Guiderius.   By heavens, I'll go.
    If you will bless me, sir, and give me leave,
    I'll take the better care, but if you will not,   45
    The hazard therefore due fall on me by
    The hands of Romans!

Arviragus.   So say I. Amen.

Belarius. No reason I, since of your lives you set
    So slight a valuation, should reserve
    My cracked one to more care. Have with you, boys!   50
    If in your country wars you chance to die,
    That is my bed too, lads, and there I'll lie.
    Lead, lead. *[aside]* The time seems long; their blood
        thinks scorn
    Till it fly out and show them princes born.   *Exeunt.*

33 *o'ergrown* bearded (?) replaced (in their thoughts) (?) 34 *questioned* i.e.
on your identity 37 *hot* lecherous 39-40 *ne'er ... heel* i.e. never had
standard riding equipment 46 *hazard ... due* danger arising from being
unblessed 48 *uf* on 50 *cracked* i.e. with age 51 *country* country's

V, i   *Enter Posthumus alone [with a bloody handkerchief].*

  Posthumus. Yea, bloody cloth, I'll keep thee, for I wished
     Thou shouldst be colored thus. You married ones,
     If each of you should take this course, how many
     Must murder wives much better than themselves
5   For wrying but a little! O Pisanio,
     Every good servant does not all commands;
     No bond but to do just ones. Gods, if you
     Should have ta'en vengeance on my faults, I never
     Had lived to put on this; so had you saved
10   The noble Imogen to repent, and struck
     Me, wretch more worth your vengeance. But alack,
     You snatch some hence for little faults; that's love,
     To have them fall no more; you some permit
     To second ills with ills, each elder worse,
15   And make them dread it, to the doers' thrift.
     But Imogen is your own. Do your best wills,
     And make me blest to obey. I am brought hither
     Among th' Italian gentry, and to fight
     Against my lady's kingdom. 'Tis enough
20   That, Britain, I have killed thy mistress; peace,
     I'll give no wound to thee. Therefore, good heavens,
     Hear patiently my purpose. I'll disrobe me
     Of these Italian weeds and suit myself
     As does a Briton peasant. So I'll fight

V, i, 3 *take this course* do as I have done 5 *wrying* erring 6 *does not* does
not carry out 7 *No bond but* he is bound only 9 *put on* instigate (?) load
myself with (?) 10 *repent* i.e. for the misdeeds he imputes to her 13 *fall*
i.e. into misconduct 14 *second* duplicate, back up *elder* i.e. later (as
if evils were becoming more 'mature' with time) 15 *them* i.e. the
doers *dread it* repent the evil course *thrift* profit, gain 23 *weeds* clothes
suit dress

Against the part I come with; so I'll die   25
For thee, O Imogen, even for whom my life
Is every breath a death; and thus, unknown,
Pitied nor hated, to the face of peril
Myself I'll dedicate. Let me make men know
More valor in me than my habits show.   30
Gods, put the strength o' th' Leonati in me.
To shame the guise o' th' world, I will begin
The fashion, less without and more within.   *Exit.*

Enter Lucius, Iachimo, and the Roman Army at one door,   V, ii
    and the Briton Army at another, Leonatus Posthumus
    following like a poor soldier. They march over and go out.
    Then enter again in skirmish Iachimo and Posthumus.
    He vanquisheth and disarmeth Iachimo and then leaves
    him.

Iachimo. The heaviness and guilt within my bosom
Takes off my manhood. I have belied a lady,
The princess of this country, and the air on't
Revengingly enfeebles me; or could this carl,
A very drudge of nature's, have subdued me   5
In my profession? Knighthoods and honors, borne
As I wear mine, are titles but of scorn.
If that thy gentry, Britain, go before
This lout as he exceeds our lords, the odds
Is that we scarce are men and you are gods.   *Exit.* 10

The battle continues. The Britons fly; Cymbeline is taken.
    Then enter, to his rescue, Belarius, Guiderius, and
    Arviragus.

25 *part* side   30 *habits show* clothes proclaim   32 *guise* practice   33 *fashion, less without* i.e. fashion of having less external show   V, ii, 2 *off* away
3 *air on't* nature of it   4 *carl* peasant   8 *go before* excel

Belarius. Stand, stand! We have th' advantage of the
    ground.
    The lane is guarded. Nothing routs us but
    The villainy of our fears.
Guiderius, Arviragus.   Stand, stand, and fight!

*Enter Posthumus, and seconds the Britons. They rescue
    Cymbeline and exeunt. Then enter Lucius, Iachimo, and
    Imogen.*

Lucius. Away, boy, from the troops, and save thyself,
15   For friends kill friends, and the disorder's such
    As war were hoodwinked.
Iachimo.   'Tis their fresh supplies.
Lucius. It is a day turned strangely; or betimes
    Let's reinforce or fly.   *Exeunt.*

V, iii   *Enter Posthumus and a Briton Lord.*

Lord. Cam'st thou from where they made the stand?
Posthumus.   I did;
    Though you, it seems, come from the fliers.
Lord.   I did.
Posthumus. No blame be to you, sir, for all was lost,
    But that the heavens fought. The King himself
5   Of his wings destitute, the army broken,
    And but the backs of Britons seen, all flying
    Through a strait lane; the enemy full-hearted,
    Lolling the tongue with slaught'ring, having work
    More plentiful than tools to do't, struck down
10   Some mortally, some slightly touched, some falling

---

16 *hoodwinked* blindfolded   17 *or* either   *betimes* in time   V, iii, 7 *strait*
narrow   *full-hearted* with high morale   8 *Lolling* letting hang out
10 *touched* wounded

Merely through fear, that the strait pass was dammed
With dead men hurt behind, and cowards living
To die with length'ned shame.
Lord.   Where was this lane?
Posthumus. Close by the battle, ditched, and walled with
    turf;
Which gave advantage to an ancient soldier,   15
An honest one I warrant, who deserved
So long a breeding as his white beard came to,
In doing this for's country. Athwart the lane
He with two striplings—lads more like to run
The country base than to commit such slaughter;   20
With faces fit for masks, or rather fairer
Than those for preservation cased or shame—
Made good the passage, cried to those that fled,
'Our Britain's harts die flying, not our men.
To darkness fleet souls that fly backwards. Stand,   25
Or we are Romans and will give you that
Like beasts which you shun beastly, and may save
But to look back in frown. Stand, stand!' These three,
Three thousand confident, in act as many—
For three performers are the file when all   30
The rest do nothing—with this word 'Stand, stand,'
Accommodated by the place, more charming
With their own nobleness, which could have turned
A distaff to a lance, gilded pale looks,

---

12 *behind* i.e. while running away 17 *breeding* life, support, cherishing
19–20 *run . . . base* play the game of prisoner's base 21 *fit for masks* delicate
enough to justify protection against the sun 22 *for . . . shame* covered for
such protection or for modesty 25 *fleet* hurry 26 *we are Romans* we shall
play the part of Romans 27 *beastly* i.e. like cowards 27–28 *save . . . frown*
prevent by looking back fiercely 30 *file* whole force 32 *Accommodated*
given an advantage *more charming* winning over others (to turn and fight)
34 *A distaff . . . lance* a housewife into a soldier *gilded* restored color to

Part shame, part spirit renewed; that some, turned
35   coward
But by example — O, a sin in war,
Damned in the first beginners! — gan to look
The way that they did and to grin like lions
Upon the pikes o' th' hunters. Then began
40   A stop i' th' chaser, a retire; anon
A rout, confusion thick. Forthwith they fly
Chickens, the way which they stooped eagles; slaves,
The strides they victors made; and now our cowards,
Like fragments in hard voyages, became
45   The life o' th' need. Having found the backdoor open
Of the unguarded hearts, heavens, how they wound!
Some slain before, some dying, some their friends
O'erborne i' th' former wave, ten chased by one
Are now each one the slaughterman of twenty.
50   Those that would die or ere resist are grown
The mortal bugs o' th' field.

Lord.   This was strange chance:
A narrow lane, an old man, and two boys.

Posthumus. Nay, do not wonder at it. You are made
Rather to wonder at the things you hear
55   Than to work any. Will you rhyme upon't
And vent it for a mock'ry? Here is one:

---

35 *Part . . . part* in some . . . in others   36 *by example* by imitating others
37 *gan* began   37–38 *look The way* face in the direction   38 *they* i.e. Belarius
and his sons   *grin* i.e. bare the teeth   40 *chaser* pursuer   *retire* retreat
42 *Chickens* like chickens   *way* route   *stooped eagles* swooped over like
eagles   *slaves* like slaves (they fly back over)   43 *victors* as victors   44 *fragments* i.e. of food   45 *life . . . need* support of life in time of need   45–46 *Having . . . hearts* i.e. having found that the Romans were not invulnerable
47 *slain* i.e. having played dead   *dying* i.e. severely wounded   *their
friends* friends of those already mentioned   50 *or ere* rather than   51 *mortal
bugs* deadly terrors (cf. 'bugbears')   55 *work any* perform such (things)
56 *vent it* air it, let it get around

'Two boys, an old man twice a boy, a lane,
Preserved the Britons, was the Romans' bane.'
Lord. Nay, be not angry, sir.
Posthumus.   'Lack, to what end?
Who dares not stand his foe, I'll be his friend;   60
For if he'll do as he is made to do,
I know he'll quickly fly my friendship too.
You have put me into rhyme,
Lord.   Farewell. You're angry.   *Exit.*
Posthumus. Still going? This is a lord! O noble misery,
To be i' th' field, and ask 'What news?' of me!   65
To-day how many would have given their honors
To have saved their carcasses, took heel to do't,
And yet died too! I, in mine own woe charmed,
Could not find Death where I did hear him groan
Nor feel him where he struck. Being an ugly monster,   70
'Tis strange he hides him in fresh cups, soft beds,
Sweet words, or hath moe ministers than we
That draw his knives i' th' war. Well, I will find him,
For being now a favorer to the Briton,
No more a Briton. I have resumed again   75
The part I came in. Fight I will no more,
But yield me to the veriest hind that shall
Once touch my shoulder. Great the slaughter is
Here made by th' Roman; great the answer be
Britons must take. For me, my ransom's death.   80

59 *'Lack* alack, alas 60 *stand* withstand 61 *as . . . do* as it is natural for
him to do 63 *put . . . rhyme* made me versify 64 *going* running away
noble misery wretchedness of a noble 68 *charmed* i.e. 'leading a charmed life'
71–72 *hides . . . words* i.e. appears from unexpected places 72 *moe* more
74 *being . . . favorer* death now favoring 76 *part . . . in* i.e. his role as a
Roman (as the way to find death, now helping the British by taking their
enemies) 77 *hind* peasant 78 *touch my shoulder* i.e. as sign of arrest
79 *answer* retaliation

On either side I come to spend my breath,
Which neither here I'll keep nor bear again,
But end it by some means for Imogen.

Enter two [Briton] Captains and Soldiers.

1. *Captain.* Great Jupiter be praised, Lucius is taken.
85 'Tis thought the old man and his sons were angels.
2. *Captain.* There was a fourth man, in a silly habit,
That gave th' affront with them.
1. *Captain.*   So 'tis reported,
But none of 'em can be found. Stand, who's there?
Posthumus. A Roman,
90 Who had not now been drooping here if seconds
Had answered him.
2. *Captain.*   Lay hands on him. A dog,
A leg of Rome shall not return to tell
What crows have pecked them here. He brags his service
As if he were of note. Bring him to th' King.

*Enter Cymbeline, Belarius, Guiderius, Arviragus, Pisanio,
and Roman Captives. The Captains present Posthumus
to Cymbeline, who delivers him over to a jailer.*

[*Exeunt.*]

V, iv   *Enter Posthumus and [two] Jailer[s].*

1. *Jailer.* You shall not now be stol'n; you have locks upon
you.
So graze as you find pasture.
2. *Jailer.*   Ay, or a stomach.

[*Exeunt Jailers.*]

81 *spend my breath* yield my life   86 *silly habit* simple garb   87 *affront*
attack   90 *seconds* supporters   91 *answered him* acted as he did

Posthumus. Most welcome, bondage, for thou art a way,
  I think, to liberty. Yet am I better
  Than one that's sick o' th' gout, since he had rather   5
  Groan so in perpetuity than be cured
  By th' sure physician, Death, who is the key
  T' unbar these locks. My conscience, thou art fettered
  More than my shanks and wrists. You good gods, give
    me
  The penitent instrument to pick that bolt,   10
  Then free for ever. Is 't enough I am sorry?
  So children temporal fathers do appease;
  Gods are more full of mercy. Must I repent,
  I cannot do it better than in gyves,
  Desired more than constrained. To satisfy,   15
  If of my freedom 'tis the main part, take
  No stricter render of me than my all.
  I know you are more clement than vile men,
  Who of their broken debtors take a third,
  A sixth, a tenth, letting them thrive again   20
  On their abatement. That's not my desire.
  For Imogen's dear life take mine; and though
  'Tis not so dear, yet 'tis a life; you coined it.
  'Tween man and man they weigh not every stamp;
  Though light, take pieces for the figure's sake;   25
  You rather mine, being yours. And so, great pow'rs,
  If you will take this audit, take this life

V, iv, 10 *penitent ... bolt* penitence to unfetter his conscience   11 *free* i.e.
in death   12 *So* i.e. by being sorry   14 *gyves* fetters   15 *constrained*
forced upon me   *satisfy* atone   16 *If ... part* if it (atonement) is essential
to my freedom (of conscience)   17 *stricter render* sterner repayment
all i.e. life   21 *abatement* reduced principal   *That* i.e. to 'thrive again'
24 *stamp* coin   25 *figure's* i.e. of the royal image on the coin   26 *You ...
yours* you more readily take my life (light coin though it is) because you
made it   27 *take* accept

And cancel these cold bonds. O Imogen,
I'll speak to thee in silence.   *[Sleeps.]*

Solemn music. Enter, as in an apparition, Sicilius Leonatus,
father to Posthumus, an old man attired like a warrior;
leading in his hand an ancient Matron, his wife and
mother to Posthumus, with music before them. Then,
after other music, follow the two young Leonati, brothers
to Posthumus, with wounds as they died in the wars. They
circle Posthumus round as he lies sleeping.

30 *Sicilius.*   No more, thou Thunder-master, show
                    Thy spite on mortal flies.
              With Mars fall out, with Juno chide,
                    That thy adulteries
                        Rates and revenges.
35   Hath my poor boy done aught but well,
                    Whose face I never saw?
            I died whilst in the womb he stayed
                    Attending nature's law;
            Whose father then, as men report
40   Thou orphans' father art,
            Thou shouldst have been, and shielded him
                    From this earth-vexing smart.

Mother.   Lucina lent not me her aid,
                    But took me in my throes,
45   That from me was Posthumus ripped,
                    Came crying 'mongst his foes,
                      A thing of pity.

---

28 *cold* heavy, depressing   30 *Thunder-master* Jupiter   33 *That* who
34 *Rates* scolds   38 *Attending nature's law* awaiting the completion of the
natural process   42 *earth-vexing smart* suffering that afflicts earthly life
43 *Lucina* goddess of childbirth

Sicilius.	Great Nature like his ancestry
	Moulded the stuff so fair
	That he deserved the praise o' th' world, 50
	As great Sicilius' heir.
1. Brother.	When once he was mature for man,
	In Britain where was he
	That could stand up his parallel,
	Or fruitful object be 55
	In eye of Imogen, that best
	Could deem his dignity?
Mother.	With marriage wherefore was he mocked,
	To be exiled and thrown
	From Leonati seat and cast 60
	From her his dearest one,
	Sweet Imogen?
Sicilius.	Why did you suffer Iachimo,
	Slight thing of Italy,
	To taint his nobler heart and brain 65
	With needless jealousy,
	And to become the geck and scorn
	O' th' other's villainy?
2. Brother.	For this from stiller seats we came,
	Our parents and us twain, 70
	That striking in our country's cause
	Fell bravely and were slain,

49 *stuff* substance (cf. I, i, 23)   52 *mature for man* grown up   55 *fruitful* fulfilling potentialities   57 *deem his dignity* judge his worth   63 *suffer* allow 64 *Slight* contemptible   65 *taint* infect   67 *geck* dupe   69 *stiller seats* quieter dwelling places (Elysium)   71 *That* who

Our fealty and Tenantius' right
With honor to maintain.

75 *1. Brother.*   Like hardiment Posthumus hath
To Cymbeline performed.
Then, Jupiter, thou king of gods,
Why hast thou thus adjourned
The graces for his merits due,
80   Being all to dolors turned?

Sicilius.   Thy crystal window ope; look out.
No longer exercise
Upon a valiant race thy harsh
And potent injuries.

85 *Mother.*   Since, Jupiter, our son is good,
Take off his miseries.

Sicilius.   Peep through thy marble mansion. Help,
Or we poor ghosts will cry
To th' shining synod of the rest
90   Against thy deity.

Brothers.   Help, Jupiter, or we appeal
And from thy justice fly.

*Jupiter descends in thunder and lightning, sitting upon an
eagle. He throws a thunderbolt. The Ghosts fall on their
knees.*

Jupiter. No more, you petty spirits of region low,

75 *hardiment* courageous deeds   78 *adjourned* put off   80 *dolors* sorrows
86 *off* away   89 *synod . . . rest* assembly of the gods

Offend our hearing. Hush! How dare you ghosts
Accuse the Thunderer, whose bolt, you know,   95
   Sky-planted, batters all rebelling coasts?
Poor shadows of Elysium, hence, and rest
   Upon your never-withering banks of flow'rs.
Be not with mortal accidents opprest.
   No care of yours it is; you know 'tis ours.   100
Whom best I love I cross; to make my gift,
   The more delayed, delighted. Be content.
Your low-laid son our godhead will uplift;
   His comforts thrive, his trials well are spent.
Our Jovial star reigned at his birth, and in   105
   Our temple was he married. Rise, and fade.
He shall be lord of Lady Imogen,
   And happier much by his affliction made.
This tablet lay upon his breast, wherein
   Our pleasure his full fortune doth confine.   110
And so, away; no farther with your din
   Express impatience, lest you stir up mine.
   Mount, eagle, to my palace crystalline.   *Ascends.*

Sicilius. He came in thunder; his celestial breath
   Was sulphurous to smell; the holy eagle   115
Stooped, as to foot us. His ascension is
More sweet than our blest fields; his royal bird
Prunes the immortal wing and cloys his beak,
As when his god is pleased.
All.   Thanks, Jupiter.
Sicilius. The marble pavement closes; he is entered   120

96 *Sky-planted* growing in the sky, based in the sky   99 *accidents* **events**
102 *delighted* (the more) delighted in   104 *spent* ended   105 *Jovial star*
planet Jupiter, supposed to bring good fortune   110 *confine* set down con-
cisely   116 *Stooped . . . foot* swooped as if to seize (with claws)   117 *More
sweet* i.e. in contrast with the sulphurous descent   118 *Prunes* trims   *cloys*
claws   120 *marble pavement* i.e. heaven

His radiant roof. Away, and, to be blest,
Let us with care perform his great behest.

                              [The Ghosts] vanish.

Posthumus. *[waking]* Sleep, thou hast been a grandsire and
    begot
    A father to me, and thou hast created
125 A mother and two brothers; but, O scorn,
    Gone! They went hence so soon as they were born.
    And so I am awake. Poor wretches that depend
    On greatness' favor, dream as I have done;
    Wake, and find nothing. But, alas, I swerve.
130 Many dream not to find, neither deserve,
    And yet are steeped in favors. So am I,
    That have this golden chance and know not why.
    What fairies haunt this ground? A book? O rare one,
    Be not, as is our fangled world, a garment
135 Nobler than that it covers. Let thy effects
    So follow to be most unlike our courtiers,
    As good as promise.   *Reads.*

    'When as a lion's whelp shall, to himself unknown,
without seeking find, and be embraced by a piece of
140 tender air; and when from a stately cedar shall be lopped
branches which, being dead many years, shall after revive,
be jointed to the old stock, and freshly grow; then shall
Posthumus end his miseries, Britain be fortunate and
flourish in peace and plenty.'
145 'Tis still a dream, or else such stuff as madmen
    Tongue, and brain not; either both, or nothing,

---

125 *O scorn* what a bitter joke 129 *swerve* err (cf. 'I'm off the track')
133 *book* i.e. the 'tablet' of l. 109 134 *fangled* dressy, fancy 135 *effects* ful-
fillment 136 *to* as to 138 *When as* when 139 *piece* creature, morsel
146 *Tongue* say *brain* understand

Or senseless speaking, or a speaking such
As sense cannot untie. Be what it is,
The action of my life is like it, which
I'll keep, if but for sympathy.   150

Enter Jailer.

Jailer. Come, sir, are you ready for death?
Posthumus. Over-roasted rather; ready long ago.
Jailer. Hanging is the word, sir. If you be ready for that,
    you are well cooked.
Posthumus. So, if I prove a good repast to the spectators,   155
    the dish pays the shot.
Jailer. A heavy reckoning for you, sir. But the comfort is,
    you shall be called to no more payments, fear no more
    tavern bills, which are often the sadness of parting, as
    the procuring of mirth. You come in faint for want of   160
    meat, depart reeling with too much drink; sorry that
    you have paid too much, and sorry that you are paid too
    much; purse and brain both empty; the brain the heavier
    for being too light, the purse too light, being drawn of
    heaviness. O, of this contradiction you shall now be quit.   165
    O, the charity of a penny cord! It sums up thousands in
    a trice. You have no true debitor and creditor but it; of
    what's past, is, and to come, the discharge. Your neck,
    sir, is pen, book, and counters; so the acquittance follows.
Posthumus. I am merrier to die than thou art to live.   170

147 *senseless* irrational   147–48 *such . . . untie* too cryptic for rational
analysis   149 *like it* i.e. in being difficult to understand   150 *sympathy* re-
semblance   153 *Hanging* (pun on death by hanging and hanging up of meat)
156 *dish* food   *shot* reckoning   159 *often* as often   162 *are paid* are paid
off, punished (by too much liquor)   164 *drawn* emptied   166 *cord* i.e. for
hanging   167 *debitor and creditor* accountant   168 *discharge* payment
169 *counters* round pieces of metal used for reckoning   *acquittance* receipt
170 *to die . . . to live* in dying . . . in living

153

Jailer. Indeed, sir, he that sleeps feels not the toothache; but
a man that were to sleep your sleep, and a hangman to
help him to bed, I think he would change places with his
officer; for look you, sir, you know not which way you
175 shall go.

Posthumus. Yes indeed do I, fellow.

Jailer. Your death has eyes in's head then. I have not
seen him so pictured. You must either be directed by
some that take upon them to know, or to take upon
180 yourself that which I am sure you do not know, or jump
the after-inquiry on your own peril. And how you shall
speed in your journey's end, I think you'll never return
to tell one.

Posthumus. I tell thee, fellow, there are none want eyes to
185 direct them the way I am going but such as wink and
will not use them.

Jailer. What an infinite mock is this, that a man should
have the best use of eyes to see the way of blindness! I
am sure hanging 's the way of winking.

Enter a Messenger.

190 *Messenger.* Knock off his manacles; bring your prisoner to
the King.

Posthumus. Thou bring'st good news; I am called to be
made free.

Jailer. I'll be hanged then.

195 *Posthumus.* Thou shalt be then freer than a jailer. No bolts
for the dead.   *Exeunt [Posthumus and Messenger].*

Jailer. Unless a man would marry a gallows and beget

172 *a man that were* as for a man scheduled 174 *officer* i.e. the hangman
178 *so pictured* i.e. in the conventional skull representing death 179 *some*
clergy (?) 179–80 *take upon yourself* decide for yourself (on your salvation)
180 *jump* gamble on 181 *after-inquiry* final judgment 182 *speed in* make
out at 185 *wink* close 187 *mock* joke 193 *made free* i.e. by death

young gibbets, I never saw one so prone. Yet, on my
conscience, there are verier knaves desire to live, for all
he be a Roman; and there be some of them too that die   200
against their wills. So should I, if I were one. I would we
were all of one mind, and one mind good. O, there were
desolation of jailers and gallowses! I speak against my
present profit, but my wish hath a preferment in't.

                                                    [Exit.]

Enter Cymbeline, Belarius, Guiderius, Arviragus, Pisanio,   V, v
    and Lords.

Cymbeline. Stand by my side, you whom the gods have
    made
Preservers of my throne. Woe is my heart
That the poor soldier that so richly fought,
Whose rags shamed gilded arms, whose naked breast
Stepped before targes of proof, cannot be found.   5
He shall be happy that can find him, if
Our grace can make him so.
Belarius.   I never saw
Such noble fury in so poor a thing,
Such precious deeds in one that promised naught
But beggary and poor looks.
Cymbeline.   No tidings of him?   10
Pisanio. He hath been searched among the dead and living,
But no trace of him.
Cymbeline.   To my grief, I am

198 *prone* inclined (to die)   204 *hath . . . in't* includes a better position
for myself   V, v, 5 *targes of proof* shields of proved strength   9 *promised*
offered, presented

The heir of his reward, *[to Belarius, Guiderius, and Arvir-*
agus] which I will add
To you, the liver, heart, and brain of Britain,
15 By whom I grant she lives. 'Tis now the time
To ask of whence you are. Report it.
Belarius.   Sir,
In Cambria are we born, and gentlemen.
Further to boast were neither true nor modest,
Unless I add we are honest.
Cymbeline.   Bow your knees.
20 Arise my knights o' th' battle; I create you
Companions to our person and will fit you
With dignities becoming your estates.

Enter Cornelius and Ladies.

There's business in these faces. Why so sadly
Greet you our victory? You look like Romans
And not o' th' court of Britain.
25 *Cornelius.*   Hail, great King!
To sour your happiness I must report
The Queen is dead.
Cymbeline.   Who worse than a physician
Would this report become? But I consider
By med'cine life may be prolonged, yet death
30 Will seize the doctor too. How ended she?
Cornelius. With horror, madly dying, like her life,
Which, being cruel to the world, concluded
Most cruel to herself. What she confessed
I will report, so please you. These her women

14 *the liver . . . brain* who are the vital parts 15 *she* Britain 20 *knights
. . . battle* knights created on the battlefield (cf. 'battlefield commission')
21 *fit* equip 22 *estates* status as knights 23 *There's . . . faces* i.e. their
looks show that these persons have something important to tell 27 *Who*
(for *whom*)

Can trip me if I err, who with wet cheeks   35
Were present when she finished.

Cymbeline.   Prithee say.

Cornelius. First, she confessed she never loved you, only
Affected greatness got by you, not you;
Married your royalty, was wife to your place,
Abhorred your person.

Cymbeline.   She alone knew this,   40
And but she spoke it dying, I would not
Believe her lips in opening it. Proceed.

Cornelius. Your daughter, whom she bore in hand to love
With such integrity, she did confess
Was as a scorpion to her sight, whose life,   45
But that her flight prevented it, she had
Ta'en off by poison.

Cymbeline.   O most delicate fiend!
Who is't can read a woman? Is there more?

Cornelius. More, sir, and worse. She did confess she had
For you a mortal mineral, which, being took,   50
Should by the minute feed on life and, ling'ring,
By inches waste you. In which time she purposed,
By watching, weeping, tendance, kissing, to
O'ercome you with her show and, in time,
When she had fitted you with her craft, to work   55
Her son into th' adoption of the crown;
But failing of her end by his strange absence,
Grew shameless desperate, opened, in despite

---

35 *trip* stop, catch   38 *Affected* desired, loved   40 *your* you as a   41 *but*
but for the fact that   42 *opening* disclosing   43 *bore in hand* pretended
47 *Ta'en off* destroyed   *delicate* subtle   50 *mortal mineral* deadly poison
51 *by the minute* minute by minute   52 *waste* consume, destroy   53 *tendance*
attentiveness   54 *show* pretense (of devotion)   55 *fitted* shaped to her
purpose   56 *adoption of* adoption by you as heir to

Of heaven and men, her purposes, repented
60   The evils she hatched were not effected, so
Despairing died.
Cymbeline.   Heard you all this, her women?
Lady. We did, so please your Highness.
Cymbeline.   Mine eyes
Were not in fault, for she was beautiful;
Mine ears, that heard her flattery; nor my heart,
65   That thought her like her seeming. It had been vicious
To have mistrusted her. Yet, O my daughter,
That it was folly in me thou mayst say,
And prove it in thy feeling. Heaven mend all!

*Enter Lucius, Iachimo, [the Soothsayer,] and other Roman
    Prisoners, [Posthumus] Leonatus behind, and Imogen.*

Thou com'st not, Caius, now for tribute. That
70   The Britons have razed out, though with the loss
Of many a bold one; whose kinsmen have made suit
That their good souls may be appeased with slaughter
Of you their captives, which ourself have granted.
So think of your estate.
75 *Lucius.* Consider, sir, the chance of war. The day
Was yours by accident; had it gone with us,
We should not, when the blood was cool, have threatened
Our prisoners with the sword. But since the gods
Will have it thus, that nothing but our lives
80   May be called ransom, let it come. Sufficeth
A Roman with a Roman's heart can suffer.
Augustus lives to think on't — and so much

59 *repented* was bitterly sorry because   65 *seeming* appearance   *had been
vicious* would have been a fault   67 *it* i.e. trusting her   68 *prove* experience
feeling suffering   70 *razed out* erased   72 *their* i.e. of those lost in battle
74 *estate* spiritual state   76 *had . . . us* had we won

For my peculiar care. This one thing only
I will entreat: my boy, a Briton born,
Let him be ransomed. Never master had   85
A page so kind, so duteous, diligent,
So tender over his occasions, true,
So feat, so nurse-like. Let his virtue join
With my request, which I'll make bold your Highness
Cannot deny. He hath done no Briton harm,   90
Though he have served a Roman. Save him, sir,
And spare no blood beside.

Cymbeline.   I have surely seen him;
His favor is familiar to me. Boy,
Thou hast looked thyself into my grace
And art mine own. I know not why, wherefore,   95
To say 'Live, boy.' Ne'er thank thy master. Live,
And ask of Cymbeline what boon thou wilt,
Fitting my bounty and thy state; I'll give it,
Yea, though thou do demand a prisoner,
The noblest ta'en.

Imogen.   I humbly thank your Highness.   100

Lucius. I do not bid thee beg my life, good lad,
And yet I know thou wilt.

Imogen.   No, no, alack,
There's other work in hand. I see a thing
Bitter to me as death; your life, good master,
Must shuffle for itself.

Lucius.   The boy disdains me;   105

---

83 *my peculiar care* care for myself   87 *tender ... occasions* sensitive to his
(master's) wants   88 *feat* skillful   92 *no blood beside* the blood of no one else
93 *favor* face   94 *looked ... grace* by your looks secured my mercy   95 *I
... wherefore* (cf. 'I don't know why I'm doing it'; hence, 'You need
not thank Lucius')   98 *Fitting* appropriate to   103 *thing* (cf. ll. 135–36)
105 *shuffle* make out as best it can

He leaves me, scorns me. Briefly die their joys
That place them on the truth of girls and boys.
Why stands he so perplexed?

Cymbeline.   What wouldst thou, boy?
I love thee more and more. Think more and more
What's best to ask. Know'st him thou look'st on?
110   Speak.
Wilt have him live? Is he thy kin? Thy friend?

Imogen. He is a Roman, no more kin to me
Than I to your Highness; who, being born your vassal,
Am something nearer.

Cymbeline.   Wherefore ey'st him so?

115 *Imogen.* I'll tell you, sir, in private, if you please
To give me hearing.

Cymbeline.   Ay, with all my heart,
And lend my best attention. What's thy name?

Imogen. Fidele, sir.

Cymbeline.   Thou'rt my good youth, my page;
I'll be thy master. Walk with me; speak freely.

                    [*Cymbeline and Imogen talk apart.*]

Belarius. Is not this boy revived from death?

120 *Arviragus.*   One sand another
Not more resembles that sweet rosy lad
Who died, and was Fidele. What think you?

Guiderius. The same dead thing alive.

Belarius. Peace, peace, see further. He eyes us not; forbear.
125   Creatures may be alike. Were't he, I am sure
He would have spoke to us.

Guiderius.   But we see him dead.

106 *Briefly* soon   106–7 *their joys That* the joys of those who   107 *place
. . . truth* make them depend on the fidelity   108 *perplexed* troubled
114 *something nearer* somewhat closer (to you than he is to me)   121 *Not
. . . lad* (unusually elliptical; some words may be lost)   126 *But . . . dead*
unless we see him dead (?) but what we see is a ghost (?)

Belarius. Be silent; let's see further.

Pisanio.   *[aside]* It is my mistress.
  Since she is living, let the time run on
  To good or bad.   *[Cymbeline and Imogen advance.]*

Cymbeline.   Come, stand thou by our side;
  Make thy demand aloud. *[to Iachimo]* Sir, step you forth,   130
  Give answer to this boy, and do it freely;
  Or, by our greatness and the grace of it,
  Which is our honor, bitter torture shall
  Winnow the truth from falsehood. — On, speak to him.

Imogen. My boon is that this gentleman may render   135
  Of whom he had this ring.

Posthumus.   *[aside]* What's that to him?

Cymbeline. That diamond upon your finger, say
  How came it yours.

Iachimo. Thou'lt torture me to leave unspoken that
  Which to be spoke would torture thee.

Cymbeline.   How? Me?   140

Iachimo. I am glad to be constrained to utter that
  Which torments me to conceal. By villainy
  I got this ring. 'Twas Leonatus' jewel,
  Whom thou didst banish, and — which more may grieve
    thee,
  As it doth me — a nobler sir ne'er lived   145
  'Twixt sky and ground. Wilt thou hear more, my lord?

Cymbeline. All that belongs to this.

Iachimo.   That paragon, thy daughter,
  For whom my heart drops blood and my false spirits
  Quail to remember — Give me leave; I faint.

132–33 *grace ... honor* our honor, which embellishes (our greatness)
135 *render* tell   139 *to leave* for leaving

Cymbeline. My daughter? What of her? Renew thy
150   strength.
I had rather thou shouldst live while nature will
Than die ere I hear more. Strive, man, and speak.
Iachimo. Upon a time — unhappy was the clock
That struck the hour! — it was in Rome — accursed
155   The mansion where! — 'twas at a feast — O, would
Our viands had been poisoned, or at least
Those which I heaved to head! — the good Posthumus —
What should I say? He was too good to be
Where ill men were, and was the best of all
160   Amongst the rar'st of good ones — sitting sadly,
Hearing us praise our loves of Italy
For beauty that made barren the swelled boast
Of him that best could speak; for feature, laming
The shrine of Venus or straight-pight Minerva,
165   Postures beyond brief nature; for condition,
A shop of all the qualities that man
Loves woman for; besides that hook of wiving,
Fairness which strikes the eye —
Cymbeline.   I stand on fire.
Come to the matter.
Iachimo.   All too soon I shall,
170   Unless thou wouldst grieve quickly. This Posthumus,
Most like a noble lord in love and one
That had a royal lover, took his hint,
And not dispraising whom we praised — therein

---

151 *while nature will* i.e. your natural life   157 *heaved to head* raised to mouth
162 *made...boast* rendered even an exaggerated boast powerless (to express)
163 *feature* figure   *laming* making a cripple of   164 *shrine* image   *straight-
pight* erect   165 *Postures* forms   *beyond brief nature* of immortal beings (?)
more enduring (as art) than natural beings (?)   *condition* character   166 *shop*
store   167 *hook* i.e. fishhook   *of wiving* for marriage   169 *matter* point
172 *lover* woman in love with him   *hint* opportunity

He was as calm as virtue — he began
His mistress' picture; which by his tongue being made,   175
And then a mind put in't, either our brags
Were cracked of kitchen trulls, or his description
Proved us unspeaking sots.
Cymbeline.   Nay, nay, to th' purpose.
Iachimo. Your daughter's chastity — there it begins.
He spake of her as Dian had hot dreams   180
And she alone were cold; whereat I, wretch,
Made scruple of his praise and wagered with him
Pieces of gold 'gainst this which then he wore
Upon his honored finger, to attain
In suit the place of's bed and win this ring   185
By hers and mine adultery. He, true knight,
No lesser of her honor confident
Than I did truly find her, stakes this ring;
And would so, had it been a carbuncle
Of Phoebus' wheel, and might so safely, had it   190
Been all the worth of's car. Away to Britain
Post I in this design. Well may you, sir,
Remember me at court, where I was taught
Of your chaste daughter the wide difference
'Twixt amorous and villainous. Being thus quenched   195
Of hope, not longing, mine Italian brain
Gan in your duller Britain operate
Most vilely; for my vantage, excellent.

---

176 *mind put in't* i.e. she had brains as well as beauty   177 *cracked of* boasted
about   *trulls* wenches   178 *unspeaking sots* inarticulate fools   *to th'
purpose* (keep) to the point   180 *as* as if   *hot* lecherous   181 *cold* chaste
182 *Made scruple of* stated disbelief in   185 *In suit* by wooing   189 *would
so* would have done so   190 *Phoebus' wheel* i.e. wheel on the sun's chariot
might so might have done so   192 *Post* hurry   194 *Of* by   195 *amorous*
faithful love   195–96 *quenched Of* cooled off in   197 *duller Britain* (northern
countries supposedly produced slower minds)   198 *vantage* profit

And, to be brief, my practice so prevailed
200   That I returned with simular proof enough
To make the noble Leonatus mad
By wounding his belief in her renown
With tokens thus and thus; averring notes
Of chamber hanging, pictures, this her bracelet —
205   O cunning, how I got it! — nay, some marks
Of secret on her person, that he could not
But think her bond of chastity quite cracked,
I having ta'en the forfeit. Whereupon —
Methinks I see him now —

Posthumus.   *[advancing]* Ay, so thou dost,
210   Italian fiend! Ay me, most credulous fool,
Egregious murderer, thief, anything
That's due to all the villains past, in being,
To come! O, give me cord or knife or poison,
Some upright justicer! Thou, King, send out
215   For torturers ingenious. It is I
That all th' abhorrèd things o' th' earth amend
By being worse than they. I am Posthumus,
That killed thy daughter — villain-like, I lie —
That caused a lesser villain than myself,
220   A sacrilegious thief, to do't. The temple
Of virtue was she; yea, and she herself.
Spit, and throw stones, cast mire upon me, set
The dogs o' th' street to bay me; every villain
Be called Posthumus Leonatus, and
225   Be villainy less than 'twas! O Imogen!
My queen, my life, my wife! O Imogen,

199 *practice* scheming   200 *simular* simulated   202 *renown* good name
203 *averring notes* affirming the marks   207 *cracked* broken   208 *ta'en the
forfeit* gained what was forfeited (by breach of bond)   211 *anything* i.e. any
name   214 *justicer* judge   216 *amend* make (seem) better   221 *she herself* virtue herself   225 *Be . . . 'twas* i.e. I have made other villainies seem smaller

Imogen, Imogen!

Imogen.   Peace, my lord. Hear, hear —

Posthumus. Shall's have a play of this? Thou scornful page,
There lie thy part.   *[Thrusts her away; she falls.]*

Pisanio.   O gentlemen, help!
Mine and your mistress! O my lord Posthumus,   230
You ne'er killed Imogen till now. Help, help!
Mine honored lady!

Cymbeline.   Does the world go round?

Posthumus. How come these staggers on me?

Pisanio.   Wake, my mistress!

Cymbeline. If this be so, the gods do mean to strike me
To death with mortal joy.

Pisanio.   How fares my mistress?   235

Imogen. O, get thee from my sight;
Thou gav'st me poison. Dangerous fellow, hence;
Breathe not where princes are.

Cymbeline.   The tune of Imogen!

Pisanio. Lady,
The gods throw stones of sulphur on me if   240
That box I gave you was not thought by me
A precious thing; I had it from the Queen.

Cymbeline. New matter still.

Imogen.   It poisoned me.

Cornelius.   O gods!
I left out one thing which the Queen confessed,
Which must approve thee honest. 'If Pisanio   245
Have,' said she, 'given his mistress that confection
Which I gave him for cordial, she is served

228 *Shall's* shall we   229 *There . . . part* lying there is your role   233 *staggers* dizziness, agitation   235 *mortal* fatal   238 *tune* voice   240 *stones
of sulphur* thunderbolts   242 *precious* beneficial   243 *matter* developments
245 *approve* prove   *honest* truthful   246 *confection* mixture

As I would serve a rat.'

Cymbeline.   What's this, Cornelius?

Cornelius. The Queen, sir, very oft importuned me
250   To temper poisons for her, still pretending
        The satisfaction of her knowledge only
        In killing creatures vile, as cats and dogs
        Of no esteem. I, dreading that her purpose
        Was of more danger, did compound for her
255   A certain stuff which, being ta'en, would cease
        The present pow'r of life, but in short time
        All offices of nature should again
        Do their due functions. Have you ta'en of it?

Imogen. Most like I did, for I was dead.

Belarius.   My boys,
        There was our error.

260 *Guiderius.*   This is sure Fidele.

Imogen. Why did you throw your wedded lady from you?
        Think that you are upon a rock, and now
        Throw me again.   [*Embraces him.*]

Posthumus.   Hang there like fruit, my soul,
        Till the tree die!

Cymbeline.   How now, my flesh, my child?
265   What, mak'st thou me a dullard in this act?
        Wilt thou not speak to me?

Imogen.   [*kneeling*] Your blessing, sir.

Belarius. [*to Guiderius and Arviragus*] Though you did love
        this youth, I blame ye not;

---

250 *temper* mix   *pretending* alleging as her purpose   253 *esteem* value
254 *of more danger* more harmful   255 *cease* cut off   257 *offices of nature*
bodily parts   259 *like* probably   *dead* as if dead   262 *rock* i.e. firm
ground (?) (sometimes emended to 'lock' and explained as a metaphor from
wrestling)   263 *Throw me again* i.e. if you can (we are now inseparable)
265 *dullard* i.e. by ignoring me (and giving me no lines to speak)   *act*
perhaps, play (cf. ll. 228–29)

You had a motive for't.
Cymbeline.   My tears that fall
Prove holy water on thee. Imogen,
Thy mother's dead.
Imogen.   I am sorry for't, my lord.   270
Cymbeline. O, she was naught, and long of her it was
That we meet here so strangely; but her son
Is gone, we know not how nor where.
Pisanio.   My lord,
Now fear is from me, I'll speak troth. Lord Cloten,
Upon my lady's missing, came to me   275
With his sword drawn, foamed at the mouth, and swore,
If I discovered not which way she was gone,
It was my instant death. By accident
I had a feignèd letter of my master's
Then in my pocket, which directed him   280
To seek her on the mountains near to Milford;
Where, in a frenzy, in my master's garments,
Which he enforced from me, away he posts
With unchaste purpose and with oath to violate
My lady's honor. What became of him   285
I further know not.
Guiderius.   Let me end the story:
I slew him there.
Cymbeline.   Marry, the gods forfend!
I would not thy good deeds should from my lips
Pluck a hard sentence. Prithee, valiant youth,
Deny't again.
Guiderius.   I have spoke it, and I did it.   290

268 *motive* cause 271 *naught* evil *long of* because of 274 *troth* truth
277 *discovered* revealed 279 *letter* (cf. III, v, 99–100) 287 *forfend* forbid
288 *thy good deeds* (that after) thy good deeds (against the Romans, thou)
290 *again* against (what you have just said)

Cymbeline. He was a prince.

Guiderius. A most incivil one. The wrongs he did me
    Were nothing princelike, for he did provoke me
    With language that would make me spurn the sea
295 If it could so roar to me. I cut off's head,
    And am right glad he is not standing here
    To tell this tale of mine.

Cymbeline.   I am sorrow for thee.
    By thine own tongue thou art condemned and must
    Endure our law. Thou'rt dead.

Imogen.   That headless man
    I thought had been my lord.

300 *Cymbeline.*   Bind the offender
    And take him from our presence.

Belarius.   Stay, sir King.
    This man is better than the man he slew,
    As well descended as thyself, and hath
    More of thee merited than a band of Clotens
305 Had ever scar for. *[to the Guard]* Let his arms alone;
    They were not born for bondage.

Cymbeline.   Why, old soldier,
    Wilt thou undo the worth thou art unpaid for
    By tasting of our wrath? How of descent
    As good as we?

Arviragus.   In that he spake too far.

Cymbeline. And thou shalt die for't.

310 *Belarius.*   We will die all three
    But I will prove that two on's are as good
    As I have given out him. My sons, I must

---

297 *tell ... mine* i.e. report that he cut off my head *sorrow* (a possible idiom; some editors emend to *sorry*) 305 *Had ... for* earned by battle wounds 310 *thou* i.e. Belarius 311 *But* unless

For mine own part unfold a dangerous speech,
Though haply well for you.
Arviragus.   Your danger's ours.
Guiderius. And our good his.
Belarius.   Have at it then. By leave,   315
Thou hadst, great King, a subject who
Was called Belarius.
Cymbeline.   What of him? He is
A banished traitor.
Belarius.   He it is that hath
Assumed this age; indeed a banished man,
I know not how a traitor.
Cymbeline.   Take him hence.   320
The whole world shall not save him.
Belarius.   Not too hot.
First pay me for the nursing of thy sons,
And let it be confiscate all, so soon
As I have received it.
Cymbeline.   Nursing of my sons?
Belarius. I am too blunt and saucy; here's my knee.   325
Ere I arise I will prefer my sons;
Then spare not the old father. Mighty sir,
These two young gentlemen that call me father
And think they are my sons are none of mine;
They are the issue of your loins, my liege,   330
And blood of your begetting.
Cymbeline.   How? My issue?
Belarius. So sure as you your father's. I, old Morgan,
Am that Belarius whom you sometime banished.

313 *For ... speech* make an explanatory statement dangerous to myself
315 *Have at it* let's go ahead *By leave* by your permission 319 *Assumed
this age* taken on this look of age 321 *hot* hasty 323 *it* the payment
325 *saucy* direct, 'fresh' 326 *prefer* advance 333 *sometime* once

Your pleasure was my mere offense, my punishment
335 Itself, and all my treason; that I suffered
Was all the harm I did. These gentle princes —
For such and so they are — these twenty years
Have I trained up; those arts they have as I
Could put into them. My breeding was, sir, as
340 Your Highness knows. Their nurse, Euriphile,
Whom for the theft I wedded, stole these children
Upon my banishment. I moved her to't,
Having received the punishment before
For that which I did then. Beaten for loyalty
345 Excited me to treason. Their dear loss,
The more of you 'twas felt, the more it shaped
Unto my end of stealing them. But, gracious sir,
Here are your sons again, and I must lose
Two of the sweet'st companions in the world.
350 The benediction of these covering heavens
Fall on their heads like dew, for they are worthy
To inlay heaven with stars.

Cymbeline.   Thou weep'st and speak'st.
The service that you three have done is more
Unlike than this thou tell'st. I lost my children;
355 If these be they, I know not how to wish
A pair of worthier sons.

Belarius.   Be pleased awhile.
This gentleman whom I call Polydore,
Most worthy prince, as yours, is true Guiderius;
This gentleman, my Cadwal, Arviragus,
360 Your younger princely son. He, sir, was lapped

334–35 *Your . . . treason* my whole offense, etc., existed only because it
pleased you (to declare them) 338 *arts* accomplishments 342 *moved* incited
344 *Beaten* being beaten 346 *of* by 346–47 *shaped . . . of* served my end in
353 *service* i.e. in battle 354 *Unlike* improbable 360 *lapped* wrapped

In a most curious mantle, wrought by th' hand
Of his queen mother, which for more probation
I can with ease produce.
Cymbeline.   Guiderius had
Upon his neck a mole, a sanguine star;
It was a mark of wonder.
Belarius.   This is he,   365
Who hath upon him still that natural stamp.
It was wise Nature's end in the donation
To be his evidence now.
Cymbeline.   O, what am I?
A mother to the birth of three? Ne'er mother
Rejoiced deliverance more. Blest pray you be,   370
That, after this strange starting from your orbs,
You may reign in them now! O Imogen,
Thou hast lost by this a kingdom.
Imogen.   No, my lord,
I have got two worlds by't. O my gentle brothers,
Have we thus met? O, never say hereafter   375
But I am truest speaker. You called me brother
When I was but your sister, I you brothers
When we were so indeed.
Cymbeline.   Did you e'er meet?
Arviragus. Ay, my good lord.
Guiderius.   And at first meeting loved,
Continued so until we thought he died.   380
Cornelius. By the Queen's dram she swallowed.
Cymbeline.   O rare instinct!
When shall I hear all through? This fierce abridgment

361 *curious* artfully wrought 362 *probation* proof 364 *sanguine* blood-
red 367 *end* purpose *donation* endowing (him with the mark) 368 *his*
evidence evidence of his identity 371 *orbs* orbits 382 *fierce abridgment*
extraordinary pastime

Hath to it circumstantial branches, which
Distinction should be rich in. Where, how lived you?
385   And when came you to serve our Roman captive?
How parted with your brothers? How first met them?
Why fled you from the court? And whither? These,
And your three motives to the battle, with
I know not how much more, should be demanded,
390   And all the other by-dependences
From chance to chance; but nor the time nor place
Will serve our long interrogatories. See,
Posthumus anchors upon Imogen,
And she like harmless lightning throws her eye
395   On him, her brothers, me, her master, hitting
Each object with a joy; the counterchange
Is severally in all. Let's quit this ground
And smoke the temple with our sacrifices.
[To Belarius] Thou art my brother; so we'll hold thee
          ever.
400 *Imogen.* You are my father too, and did relieve me
To see this gracious season.
Cymbeline.   All o'erjoyed
Save these in bonds; let them be joyful too,
For they shall taste our comfort.
Imogen.   My good master,
I will yet do you service.
Lucius.   Happy be you!

---

383 *branches* ramifications, details   383–84 *which … in* which, as they
are distinguished, should be plentiful   388 *your three motives* what impelled you three   390 *by-dependences* related matters   391 *chance* happen-
ing   392 *Will serve* are suited to   396 *counterchange* exchange   397 *Is …
all* i.e. all engage in it, each according to his relationship to the others
398 *smoke* fill with incense   399 *hold* regard   400 *You* i.e. Belarius
relieve aid   401 *gracious season* joyful occasion   403 *taste our comfort* share
in our well-being

Cymbeline. The forlorn soldier, that so nobly fought,   405
  He would have well becomed this place and graced
  The thankings of a king.

Posthumus.   I am, sir,
  The soldier that did company these three
  In poor beseeming; 'twas a fitment for
  The purpose I then followed. That I was he,   410
  Speak, Iachimo. I had you down and might
  Have made you finish.

Iachimo.   *[kneeling]* I am down again,
  But now my heavy conscience sinks my knee,
  As then your force did. Take that life, beseech you,
  Which I so often owe; but your ring first,   415
  And here the bracelet of the truest princess
  That ever swore her faith.

Posthumus.   Kneel not to me.
  The pow'r that I have on you is to spare you;
  The malice towards you to forgive you. Live,
  And deal with others better.

Cymbeline.   Nobly doomed!   420
  We'll learn our freeness of a son-in-law:
  Pardon's the word to all.

Arviragus.   You holp us, sir,
  As you did mean indeed to be our brother.
  Joyed are we that you are.

Posthumus. Your servant, princes. Good my lord of Rome,   425
  Call forth your soothsayer. As I slept, methought
  Great Jupiter, upon his eagle backed,
  Appeared to me, with other spritely shows

405 *forlorn* missing   409 *beseeming* appearance (i.e garb)   *fitment for* garb fitted for   410 *followed* was carrying out   412 *finish* die   413 *sinks* makes bend   415 *often* many times (because of the extent of my misdeeds)   420 *doomed* judged   421 *freeness* generosity   424 *you are* i.e. our brother   427 *upon . . . backed* on the back of his eagle   428 *spritely shows* ghostly visions

Of mine own kindred. When I waked, I found
430   This label on my bosom, whose containing
      Is so from sense in hardness that I can
      Make no collection of it. Let him show
      His skill in the construction.

Lucius.   Philarmonus!
Soothsayer. Here, my good lord.
Lucius.   Read, and declare the meaning.
435 *Soothsayer.* *[reads]* 'When as a lion's whelp shall, to him-
      self unknown, without seeking find, and be embraced by
      a piece of tender air; and when from a stately cedar shall
      be lopped branches which, being dead many years, shall
      after revive, be jointed to the old stock, and freshly grow;
440   then shall Posthumus end his miseries, Britain be fortu-
      nate and flourish in peace and plenty.'
      [To Leonatus] Thou, Leonatus, art the lion's whelp;
      The fit and apt construction of thy name,
      Being *Leo-natus,* doth import so much.
      [To Cymbeline] The piece of tender air, thy virtuous
445   daughter,
      Which we call 'mollis aer,' and 'mollis aer'
      We term it 'mulier'; which 'mulier' I divine
      Is this most constant wife, who even now
      Answering the letter of the oracle,
      [To Posthumus] Unknown to you, unsought, were
450   clipped about
      With this most tender air.

Cymbeline.   This hath some seeming.

430 *label* piece of paper *containing* contents 431 *from . . . hardness* hard
to understand 432 *collection* elucidation 433 *construction* construing, in-
terpreting (of it) 444 *Leo-natus* lion-born *import* mean, imply 446 *mollis
aer* tender air (a supposed origin of *mulier,* woman) 449 *Answering* according to 450 *were clipped about* i.e. you were embraced (the passage is
grammatically incoherent) 451 *seeming* plausibility

Soothsayer. The lofty cedar, royal Cymbeline,
   Personates thee, and thy lopped branches point
   Thy two sons forth; who, by Belarius stol'n,
   For many years thought dead, are now revived,   455
   To the majestic cedar joined, whose issue
   Promises Britain peace and plenty.
Cymbeline.   Well,
   My peace we will begin. And, Caius Lucius,
   Although the victor, we submit to Caesar
   And to the Roman empire, promising   460
   To pay our wonted tribute, from the which
   We were dissuaded by our wicked queen,
   Whom heavens in justice, both on her and hers,
   Have laid most heavy hand.
Soothsayer. The fingers of the pow'rs above do tune   465
   The harmony of this peace. The vision
   Which I made known to Lucius ere the stroke
   Of this yet scarce-cold battle, at this instant
   Is full accomplished; for the Roman eagle,
   From south to west on wing soaring aloft,   470
   Lessened herself and in the beams o' th' sun
   So vanished; which foreshowed our princely eagle,
   Th' imperial Caesar, should again unite
   His favor with the radiant Cymbeline,
   Which shines here in the west.
Cymbeline.   Laud we the gods,   475
   And let our crooked smokes climb to their nostrils
   From our blest altars. Publish we this peace
   To all our subjects. Set we forward; let

---

453 *Personates* stands for   453–54 *point . . . forth* indicate   456 *issue* descendants   463 *Whom* on whom   *hers* i.e. Cloten   466 *vision* (cf. IV, ii, 346 ff.)   475 *Laud* praise   476 *crooked* curling   478 *Set we forward* let us march

A Roman and a British ensign wave
480 Friendly together. So through Lud's town march,
And in the temple of great Jupiter
Our peace we'll ratify, seal it with feasts.
Set on there! Never was a war did cease,
Ere bloody hands were washed, with such a peace.

Exeunt.

483 *Set on there* forward march